CLUELESS
in
NEW ORLEANS

Adventures in Adolescence

JACK SAUX

Arthur Hardy *Enterprises* INC

Published by
Arthur Hardy Enterprises, Inc.
230 Devon Drive
Mandeville, LA 70448

Copyright © 2011 by Arthur Hardy Enterprises, Inc.

All Rights Reserved

Printed in the United States of America

ISBN 978-0-930892-33-3

Art Director—David Johnson

Cover Illustrator—Yvonne Saux

About The Cover

Like most things in New Orleans, there is a story involved. I had an idea of what I wanted for a cover. I believe it is a scientific fact that women mature faster than men, and so it is
Cheryl who leads Dué from boyhood to adolescence. The presence of a blindfold shows he has
no idea of his location or destination—perhaps a fair definition of "clueless." The pogo stick
demonstrates that his course is more random than direct.

The process of transforming my thoughts into a cover started with our good friend
Jennifer Adams. She put away her law books and spent a morning in our beautiful City Park,
taking pictures of Claire Bear. Bear was selected because she is the right size and the camera
loves her. Claire did a bit of research and learned that green is a leadership color. And like
Cheryl, her outfit was coordinated, her shoes matched her shirt. The choice for the boy on the
pogo stick was easy. I have a grandson who is not only the correct age, but only Ben would be
eager to ride a pogo stick while blindfolded. David Johnson, art director without equal, put all
of the ideas and photos into a sketch, which my talented wife, Yvonne, turned into a pastel.

The streetcar and lamppost ideas are courtesy of my publisher turned friend, Arthur
Hardy, cheerleader and ambassador for all things New Orleans.

A Special Thanks

A committee cannot write a book. The old story is that a camel is a horse designed by a
committee. But, without the suggestions and ideas of my "focus" group, *Clueless* would have
been very different. To the group, twenty females aged 10 to well north of 70, thanks.

For editorial assistance—Stephanie, Susan, Jason, and Sharon, thanks.

For the cover, thank you Yvonne and David.

And a special thanks to Arthur.

DEDICATION

To my children and grandchildren,

Your lives and experiences are the fuel for my imagination.

Love, Poppeeee!

Chapter 1

My childhood ended a week after my 12th birthday—seven action-packed days. I planned and initiated a covert operation. The mission fell short of its objective and there was collateral damage—my best friend's collarbone. I made an initial foray into the complicated world of male-female relationships. The neighborhood bully used my face for a speed bag, and my naiveté almost killed my dad.

And on the night when I witnessed the event that ended my childhood, I committed an unforgivable sin.

I can't find fault with the way the week opened. My birthday was cool. Dad gave me two gifts. He had taken my bike to the shop on Tulane Avenue for a custom paint job, and he had installed the most incredible light ever on the front fender—a light that never needed batteries.

Dad and I lived in half of a shotgun double, an architectural style which is all New Orleans. My two great aunts, Rose and Na-ne, owned the house and lived on the other side. Dad and I had moved there right after mom's accident.

Yeah, this is New Orleans. People drink and then they drive. Mom was on her way home from work, waiting at the bus stop, when the drunk driver hit her. My aunts helped Dad with me.

For the birthday, even though it was not the season for it, those two sweet old ladies had baked my favorite, a king cake. They had also placed a crisp five-dollar bill on my pillow.

My tribe—we weren't cool enough to be considered a gang—had pitched in to treat me to a movie, a movie that had given me an interesting idea as to how to increase our limited knowledge of anatomy.

Chapter 2

There was a time when the Ninth Ward in New Orleans was a nice place to live. Everyone was poor, not starving poor, but no extra money for frills. A family with a reliable car was considered upper class. And since none of us knew anyone with real money, we had no frame of reference to ignite feelings of jealousy or envy.

There were four members of the tribe. I suppose Jimmy was the leader. He had an older brother who knew everything in the world, especially about girls. He shared that information with Jimmy, and it got passed to us.

Fat Tony was my best friend. Yeah, we actually called him that. As a little kid, he had been sick and confined to bed for a year. Like me, he was Italian, only he had a huge family—two younger brothers, a mom, a dad, and God knows how many aunts lived with them. Everyone felt sorry for him. So what do Italians do? They fed him. Fat Tony was ounces away from having his own zip code.

Mick, the Irish member of the tribe, brought two things to the party. He had a temper that was an awesome thing to behold. When angry, he seemed to grow in size and was known to have kicked the asses of taller, older, and bigger kids. He had a sister who we'll discuss later.

Me, I'm Dué—Italian for *two*. If you are not Italian, the word is pronounced sort of like *Do a*. My dad is Pietro Bonogura. My dad's father was the first Anthony Bonogura. Since I am named after my grandfather, I am Anthony Bonogura II. But my mom was not happy with her son being called *Secundo,* so they went with *Dué.*

The movie the tribe took me to for my birthday was about submarines in World War II. None of us was interested in being a war hero on a sub—hot, sweaty, getting blown to bits by depth charges, and no women. Not what you would call a recruiting flick.

But the time was not wasted. We learned about the periscope! A tube with properly placed mirrors could see around corners. The prospects set fire to the imagination.

This brings the story to Mick's sister, Colleen. Mick was sort of an accident. Years later we learned that Catholics are prone to such accidents. At the time, it seemed strange that Colleen was 10 years older than Mick.

To say that Colleen was an attractive redhead was like saying Mardi Gras was a nice party. Her hair was somewhere between red and blonde. I can't describe it, but I still remember. And, there was a lot more to the vision than just her hair.

Colleen worked at Whitney Bank. At the first cool snap, she wore sweaters to work. We knew nothing of meteorology, but we prayed for the passage of cold fronts.

During that period in women's fashion, undergarments, more specifically brassieres, were structured so as to create perfectly symmetrical shapes. Years later, when I studied geometry at LSU and came to the chapter on cones, I closed my eyes and smiled at the memory of Colleen's geometry.

If you were to look at Mick's house from the vacant lot on the side, you would notice that all of the windows were the same height above the ground—except the bathroom window which was elevated for privacy. The screen on that window stuck out like a half-bubble. This was to allow you to tilt the window to let steam escape from the room—and to prevent guys like us from peeking inside. People also used the space as a kind of drying shelf.

We had been sitting under the tree in the lot next to Mick's when Colleen came home. She waved to us. We waved to her. Conversation died while we watched and dreamed. She walked into the house.

As if we needed more ammunition for our fantasies, Mick said, "Now, she'll take her bath. Nobody can use the damn hot water in the afternoon to make sure that Princess Friggin' Colleen has plenty of hot water for her bath."

I sat there, trying my best to picture that moment—Colleen in the bath. I stared at the elevated screen, prayed for x-ray vision, and had a brilliant thought. I looked at the screen, glanced at the tree, remembered the periscope in the submarine movie and smiled. We could do this.

"Mick," I said. "Have you ever seen your sister naked?"

He turned to me, ready to fight. "Careful, Dué, what do you think I am, some sort of perv?"

I raised my hands in a defensive posture. "No, pal! It is just that she is so fine. I was sort of wondering."

"I don't mean to get all holy on you, Dué, but looking at a guy's sister and thinking like that, well, I'd bet the nuns would call that a sin."

I had never known Mick to travel that road. I played my ace card. "Hey, Mick, if God didn't want us to look, why did he make her so fine!"

He gave the grin that would carry him through many of life's problems and whispered, "Did see her in her bra once. Friggin' awesome."

I raised my hands again in anticipation of another attack. "Now don't get mad. It's just a question. Would you mind if the rest of us saw her?" Here it was—my first effort at a leadership role in the tribe. If I could deliver, the three of them would follow me like trained seals in a circus act.

"What the frick do you mean?" Our vocabulary skills had not yet progressed to the level where the "super-f" could roll off our lips as a natural part of conversation. Mick, however, had successfully completed the first step in the process—the ability to include some form of the word "frick" as a noun, verb, gerund, or adjective in most of his sentences.

I pointed my right hand to the bathroom window, my left hand to the tree. "Remember the movie? What if we could sort of do like that periscope thing—rig a couple of mirrors in the bathroom, one on the screen and another one in the tree."

I paused to let them follow the logic.

I saw smiles. Fat Tony nodded. Jimmy said, "Could work."

Mick said, "You guys are frickin' sick."

"Anybody disagree with Mick on that?" I looked to the rest of the tribe, saw more smiles, and continued. "Cool, Mick, I understand. She's your sister. You're stopping us."

He produced his grin. "Didn't exactly say that—the thing is I could get in trouble if you all got caught."

It was my turn to smile. "So how much is that trouble worth?"

"Buck a piece, three bucks."

"Shit, Mick. That's a lot of money to look at a mirror in a tree."

Jimmy was a born negotiator.

Mick was hungry. "Special for my friends, two bucks for the three of you."

Before anyone could reply, Fat Tony entered the conversation. "To see Colleen naked? Boys, I'll cover it."

I'll never know why I did not go into sales. Then again, convincing my buddies that we had a chance to see Colleen naked could hardly be considered a tough sell.

If there had been speed limits for bicycles, on the following day we would have broken all of them on the way home from school. We had to be in place, mirrors rigged and ready, before Colleen got home.

Part of the negotiation was that Mick would help set it up. He sat in the tub. Jimmy adjusted the mirrors in the bathroom. I called directions from the tree: "Little to the left, now tilt it down."

Once the initial positioning was complete, we tweaked the angle of Fat Tony's mirror. The tree was not very big—no way would it support his weight. He would have to view from the ground.

Colleen arrived on schedule. We were in position under the tree, doing our best to appear casual. She waved. We waved. She walked into her house.

We were up that tree faster than chimps at the zoo. Colleen entered the bathroom and turned on the water. Jimmy and I sat on the limb, eyes locked on our mirror.

Fat Tony watched from ground level. "Dué," he whispered, "move it just a little left."

I did.

"Cool," I heard him say.

Her back was to our mirror when she pulled off the sweater. My throat was dry. She made some heart-stopping moves as she got out of the slip. She was covered with freckles. If my throat had been any drier, I could have spit sand. She reached behind her back for the snaps on her bra.

I'll never know whether it was our combined weight or the beating of our hearts that created the fatal vibration in the tree limb. All I know for sure is that two things broke. The limb was first, followed seconds later by Fat Tony's collarbone when we landed on him. His scream of pain ended our Peeping Tom careers.

Chapter 3

In New Orleans—and so many descriptions and explanations start with that phrase—schools were different. Most of the people in the city were Catholic, at least most of the ones I knew. Grammar schools were co-ed, but they separated us in high school. Dad said it was "a focus thing."

The separation hardly kept us from discussing, much less focusing on, the opposite sex. Young women like Colleen were a source of constant fascination. Girls our own age, seventh graders—well, there was no driving force compelling us to have much to do with them. To be precise, that was the attitude at the start of the year. As the months rolled by, there were changes. I am smiling as the words hit the page: changes in us and big changes in them. Chicken or the egg?

Her name was Cheryl Anne. Her parents used both names. We do that a lot here. Cheryl was the best athlete, male or female, in our school. Basketball was her sport. She was so quick you didn't realize she had moved. And, she could sink free throws until you got tired of counting. A skinny girl with dark brown hair. If Mick's sister Colleen's contribution to geometry was the curve, Cheryl's was the straight line.

Cheryl had gotten very sick at the end of the summer and had missed the first few weeks of school. The nuns had wanted to hold her back on account of missing so many days, but her mom and dad had refused to consider it. And that was something new in my life: people arguing with nuns and winning.

As Cheryl's health improved to the point that she could concentrate and study, Sister Mary Dominic—all of the nuns had Mary as a first name—assigned me the task of dropping off books and assignments at Cheryl's house.

I don't know how else to say this: I am good at math. Just as Cheryl's family had hoped basketball would open doors for her, my dad felt that math would be my ticket.

11

Cheryl was bright and didn't break a sweat catching up on her classes—all but math. Somehow, after she returned to school, those book and lesson drop-offs evolved into math tutoring sessions. It was my first real job.

I will never forget the day her mom pushed an envelope across the table.

"What's this?" I asked.

"Dué, you take time out of your life to help Cheryl Anne in math. You deserve compensation."

"I thought the cookies were the compensation," I said, as I pushed the envelope back toward her.

"Dué, if you do not take this," she picked up the envelope and crammed it into my shirt pocket, "I will have to find another math whiz to help Cheryl Anne—one who likes oatmeal cookies with raisins and chocolate chips."

I shook my head. "You might find somebody better at math, but nobody likes your cookies as much as I do."

We laughed.

So, once a week for the next several weeks, twice if there was a test or exam on the horizon, I would stop at their house to tutor Cheryl. It was not really tutoring, more like we were studying together. There was something else, too. I loved my dad, and he was the best, but a home without a mom is a different place. It was nice being with a complete family.

One day, as Cheryl's mom placed a plate of cookies in front of us, I saw her give Cheryl a questioning look. Cheryl shook her head. A few minutes later, in the middle of a word problem about a boat going down the river with the current, Cheryl interrupted my thoughts. "Dué, do you remember me talking about my cousin, Noel?"

I looked up from the book. "The one who lives near Tulane— the rich one?"

She nodded. "Yes. She and her parents are having a party."

"That's nice." I was back at the problem, making some notes on the paper. "A current of 10 miles an hour."

Cheryl moved my paper away. "Please, Dué, pay attention.

12

There is going to be a party for grown-ups upstairs and a party for kids downstairs."

I had no idea where this was going, but felt I should say something. "Sounds nice."

She sighed, as if I had said something wrong. In retrospect, I realize that this was my first move into the minefield of male-female relationships. My handicap was that I was using a pogo stick for transportation.

"Dué, my cousin and her friends all have boyfriends."

"Wow. And they are our age?"

Cheryl nodded.

"Well, that's different." I paused, grinned.

"What's funny?"

As good as I was in math, Cheryl was even better in literature. I said, "I believe one of the writers we studied said something about the rich being different from you and me."

She stood and applauded. "The math machine has a soul."

We laughed. I resumed work on the word problem.

She took the pencil out of my hand. "Dué, Mom says I have to go to the party, and I have to bring someone."

Progress. I finally had an idea where this was going. I offered a "thumbs up" gesture. "Cool. And since they are all boyfriend-girlfriend, you need to bring a guy."

She smiled, nodded, exhaled.

"And you want your tutor-buddy, Dué, to help you think of someone to ask."

At that point, her head dropped to the table. I thought I heard a giggle from her mom in the other room, the first of many wrong turns on the pogo stick.

She looked up and all but shouted, "Dué, will you go with me to my cousin's party?"

I offered my best apologetic look and said, "Guess I should have seen that coming."

"Like a streetcar."

I told her I would have to ask my dad.

Cheryl said we would go with her parents, and that it was not too dressy, just church clothes.

While I pedaled home, I thought about our neighborhood. Cheryl lived a short five blocks from me, but the economic distance was greater. That is not to say that the people on her street were rich, but they were certainly doing better than my neighbors. The homes on my street were doubles. Most were owner-occupied on one side with renters like Dad and me on the other. Aunt Rose and Aunt Na-ne owned our house. There were maybe three cars on my street. Every house on Cheryl's street was a single-family home, and most of them had a car in the driveway.

When I got home, Aunt Rose was cooking stew for dinner. My job was to set the table. When Dad walked in the door, Aunt Rose would appear with the food.

After grace, I opened the subject. While I was not as detailed a storyteller as Dad, I hit the basics and said Cheryl had invited me to a party at her cousin's house.

Dad smiled. "Is this a date, Dué?"

"Don't know, Dad. I've never had a date. Guess as the evening goes along, I'll figure that out."

It made me feel good to know I was such a source of entertainment to my father.

Chapter 4

Dad and I were on the front porch killing time by pulling weeds from Aunt Rose's potted plants when Cheryl's parents, Mr. and Mrs. Wolf, parked in front of our house.

I introduced the adults. They shook hands and said the nice things grown-ups say about each other's children

I pointed to the back seat. "Dad, this is Cheryl."

Dad reached through the window and extended his hand to her. As I walked around the car to get in on the other side, I heard Dad say, "I've seen you at a few of the basketball games. You have some nice shots, a real pretty one from the corner."

Holy crap! Dad was a charmer. I had never seen him like that. Cheryl actually blushed.

During the drive, Mr. and Mrs. Wolf made a few unsuccessful attempts to draw us into conversation with them. We had spent God knows how many hours next to each other studying at her kitchen table, but this was different. Cheryl and I were like prize-fighters sent to neutral corners. She hugged the door on her side, I hugged the door on mine.

In front of her cousin's house, I did a first-time thing for me—kept my opinion to myself. I had been ready to ask if they had changed the party location to a hotel. The place was huge—the biggest I had ever seen.

Mr. Wolf waved to an attendant. A wrought iron gate opened. Mr. Wolf parked where the gentleman indicated, and we followed the path to the party.

In addition to being the largest house I had ever seen in real life, it was a uniquely New Orleans-style piece of architecture called a "raised basement" house. There are no true basements here. If you dig down a foot or so, the hole fills with water. Over time, people converted the space below the main house into game rooms, guest rooms, or garages.

Noel's parents were nice. It wasn't that I expected them to be mean or anything like that, them being rich and all. I suppose I was simply surprised that they treated me like a regular person, not like a kid. Her dad suggested that Cheryl take me to see their new fish pond.

We followed the vine-covered porch around the side of the house to a set of stairs that led to an enormous garden. Everything I saw was covered with either vines or a fresh coat of white paint.

I shook my head. "Wow."

Cheryl glanced over her shoulder to make sure we were alone. "Uncle Bill is an attorney, but the money came from Aunt Sue. Her family had owned several large plantations between here and Baton Rouge."

I touched her arm—the first time I initiated physical contact.

"Cheryl, thanks for asking me. I have never been any place like this," I whispered through a half-laugh. "Probably never will again."

"Dué, if you would listen to my mother talk about how smart you are, you wouldn't say that. She thinks you will be a very successful person."

I had no idea how to respond to a compliment, so I said something about her mom wanting to keep the math tutor happy. If the look on Cheryl's face was any indication, she would have preferred that I had gone with something like "thanks."

The fish pond was bigger than my bedroom, maybe bigger than my bedroom and kitchen combined.

"Holy cow, Cheryl, look at all of those fish!"

"The big ones are koi. I think they come from Japan." She glared at me waiting for a pun.

Too impressed with the pond and its inhabitants to be stupid, I let the opportunity pass.

Her uncle also owned a place where they raised fish to sell to pet stores. Cheryl knew a lot about the different species.

Cheryl picked a spot to sit on a rock near the edge of the pond while I watched the fish and asked questions about them. After a few minutes, she said, "I guess we better go inside. Noel may be looking for us."

I stood. "Sure."

She stopped and turned to face me. "Dué, Noel is just a few months older than us, but—" she sighed, "they are sort of a fast crowd."

I had no idea where this was headed.

"Look at the windows, Dué. Do you see much light in there?"

I shook my head. It was pretty dark inside.

"Noel and her friends will be dancing or making out."

I lowered my voice as we moved closer to the door. "So what do we do? Can't we just go back to the pond, talk, and look at the fish?"

"If we don't go inside, they will think we are out here doing something wrong."

Ever see a rat in a maze? That was me—total confusion. If we stay outside and do not do anything wrong, the people inside who may be doing something wrong will think we are doing something wrong.

"I think we should go into the party and dance," Cheryl said.

I laughed. "That's easy for you to say."

"What do you mean?"

"Sounds like you can dance. I can't."

It was a wonderful moment. We looked at each other and cracked up.

"I can teach you," she said.

I looked at the ground. "That'll be kind of goofy, you giving me dance lessons."

She took my hand. "Dué, it's so dark nobody will notice. Besides, it's slow dancing. We can do it." She gave my hand a squeeze, which opened another new chapter in my life.

The room was dark, but Noel spotted us. She was sitting in a guy's lap. The two of them were curled up in a big chair by the record player.

"Thought you all had fallen into the pond." She stood, extended her hand. "Hello, I'm Noel."

Cheryl did the introduction thing. Noel's date pulled her back into his lap.

We shared a soft drink and wandered to a vacant corner of the room. Only two or three of the couples were dancing—the rest were

17

on various sofas and chairs wrapped around each other.

Cheryl whispered, "Give me your hand."

I offered my left.

She used her index finger to mark a square on my hand. Keeping her voice low, she said, "Dué, this is a box. It is what we are going to do with our feet. We start in one corner and go one-two up, one-two across, one-two down, and one-two across." She traced the pattern on my palm as she spoke.

I nodded.

"I'll whisper it to you as we move our feet. Just make very small steps and we'll be fine."

I nodded again. "Sure."

She stood in front of me and stared.

"What?" I was the rat in the maze again.

She had a sweet smile and used it. "You have to open your arms and hold me."

I hit my forehead. "Yeah, yeah, I knew that."

I opened my arms and she slipped right in there. Whoa!

Cheryl had been right. As long as I made very small steps, we did fine. Being that close—you know, dancing and all—I could smell her. It must have been perfume or something because she certainly didn't smell like that in school or at her house.

About then, weird things started to happen in my boxers. This had happened before, but never when I was near anyone else. I was glad we were not dancing too close.

"Hey," I said into her hair. It really felt nice on my face—but this led to further problems in the boxers. "Wanna take a break from all this dancing?"

She nodded and followed me to the refreshment table. We loaded up a plate to share, filled two cups with ice and split a Coke.

I glanced around the room. "Could we go outside for a while, sort of a picnic by the pond?"

"Good idea," she whispered. "I don't think we will be missed."

There was a bench across from the pond. We sat there, snacked, talked, sipped our drinks, and, as much as I hated to admit it at the time—her being a girl and all—we passed a good time.

"Guess we should go back in," she said.

"We'll see if anyone is using our place on the dance floor." As I said the words, her hand slipped into mine.

We did the dancing thing, our feet barely moving as we listened to the music—the Platters, as I recall.

At some point in time, there was a pause in our conversation, a moment when our faces were inches apart. I have no idea why or how, but my lips ended up touching hers. I felt her hand move, braced for a slap, which did not come. The hand touched my cheek and petted it while we kissed.

We sat a little closer on the ride home.

Chapter 5

Every neighborhood has a bully. We had Joey. He was perfect for the role—fat, greedy, and mean, with the I.Q. of a bus. No idea how many grades he had failed, but we were in the seventh grade, and he shaved every day.

While the rest of us were in the early stages of puberty, rumor was that Joey had "done it." Jimmy's big brother said that if Joey had done it, he had paid for it. I was not sure what that meant, but was too embarrassed to ask.

He certainly had the money to pay for whatever he wanted. A couple of days a week, he'd catch us on the way home from school. You had two options: give him whatever money you had or take a punch. His mood dictated how hard he punched—and whether he decided to stop after one.

As I was walking from the back door of the church to the bike rack after serving Mass one morning, a beautiful morning, months before the worst week ever, he grabbed me. Scared the blazes out of me, but when I saw who he was, I reached for my pocket.

He released me. "No money this time, Dué. I want to ask you something, kind of a favor."

"Oh crap," I thought. Joey being nice was not a good thing.

"Sure." I tried to sound cheerful.

"You tell anybody about this and life will get real bad for you."

"No problem."

He grabbed my arm again and applied pressure. "I know you can be a smart-ass. Don't mess with me."

I bobbed my head. "I won't tell a soul, Joey, no matter what."

"You ain't got no pimples."

Other than a discussion of grammar, I could think of nothing to say. Another rare moment. I was quiet.

"I got a lot of fucking pimples."

See how he did that? The word just flowed. Something for us to work on, but I digress. We knew he had pimples. In fact, very quietly among ourselves, we created and shared pimple jokes about him. The most recent one was from Fat Tony. "Why doesn't Joey ever smile? He's afraid some pimples will pop."

Since we had not yet entered puberty, we were exempt from maturity-related issues. A couple of us carried the exemption into later years.

"So how come I got all these fucking pimples, and you and those little fruit friends of yours don't?"

It is difficult for me to think of a day when God was kinder. All of the embarrassment, pain, and harassment Joey had inflicted on my friends and me was about to be balanced.

As I devised and walked him through a bathroom routine guaranteed to prevent and remove pimples, I should have been afraid, fearful he would realize I was setting him up and would smash me like a penny on the streetcar track. I was not fearless, but I was clever. If I could not outsmart him, I did not deserve to live.

When I finished, he gave me a hard look. "You're shitting me, you little fruit."

I set the hook. "Joey, I ain't brave. If I wasn't sure this worked, do you think I'd have the guts to tell you?"

He grabbed me by the throat. "You tell anybody about this and you're fucking dead."

"I won't tell anyone, but when your skin clears up, they'll know."

Sold! It was difficult not to dance on the way home. If I was lucky, he'd continue to perform the morning ablution until he got married or drafted into the military. By then I'd be far away and safe. "It wouldn't hurt to change my name," I thought.

The only downside of the prank was that it could not be shared. The danger that a misplaced smile or glance could end my life was too great. No, I'd have to be content with a morning vision. A picture of Joey, the terror of the neighborhood, applying nature's astringent to a washcloth and patting that on his face. "And Joey, be sure to wait five minutes before washing it off."

I pedaled past Dad on his way to the bus stop. "Good to see you start the day with a smile, son."

"It's a great day, Dad."

"Make every day a great day, Dué."

"Gonna try," I answered.

Though there was no perceptible improvement in Joey's complexion, we coexisted peacefully for nearly three months. Then one day I turned the corner on to Lavender Street to find Jimmy standing in front of my house with a cut lip and a pretty unhappy look about him.

"Jimmy, what happened?"

"Get in the house, Dué. Quick!"

I reached inside my shirt for the house key kept on the chain with my St. Christopher medal, twisted the key in the lock, and opened the door.

Jimmy pushed me into the house and slammed the door behind us. "Pack some clothes, Dué. You got to leave the neighborhood."

"What's going on, Jimmy?"

"Joey." He touched his lip. "He was waiting for you after Mass. When I came out, he punched me in the mouth. He's gonna frickin' kill you."

I smiled.

"You nuts, man? Why the hell are you smiling?"

I knew I was in trouble, but for the moment, life was sweet. "Did he tell you why he was looking for me?"

"No, Dué. He just said you were dead. I never seen him so mad."

"Jimmy, let me tell you why he's mad."

I did.

Jimmy's look of concern faded and was replaced by the hint of a smile, followed by laughter. "You mean he has been pissing on a wash cloth and patting it on his pimple-face for months?"

I nodded. "Think so. Guess someone in his family must have caught him." We were laughing so hard it was difficult to stand. Slowly, but with increasing clarity, reality set in.

I was in trouble.

Jimmy and I developed a plan. I threw some clothes in a gym bag and wrote a note to my dad. I told him I was riding my bike to Grandma's house to spend the night. My thought was that if I stayed with Grandma and Pappy for a couple of days, Joey would have time to cool off. Maybe he would even come around to seeing the humor of the whole thing. I was and remain an optimist.

The plan fell apart a block from my house. Joey broadsided me on his bike. Before I could get up to run away, he was on me—punching, kicking. He was so angry he was crying. I looked into his tear-filled, red-rimmed eyes, and for the first time in my young life, I knew fear. I did not know it was possible to punch and kick a person at the same time. There was no fighting back. I tucked into a ball-like fetal position as the punishment continued.

There was shouting in the background. An adult voice, thank God. I heard slapping sounds above Joey's shouts of rage. The kicks and blows stopped.

I peeked from under my arm. There was Mr. Stahel with a rake in his hand. I was lucky. The attack had happened in front of the home of the only person in the neighborhood who was not afraid of Joey. What made it more interesting was that Mr. Stahel was a slightly built man, definitely smaller than Joey. He spoke to me in a gentle voice. "Don't move, young man. My wife will be here in a minute." He did not know my name, but he had confronted Joey to help me. I would never forget that act of kindness and bravery.

Joey muttered a profanity.

Mr. Stahel turned to face him, held the rake like a bat. "Don't make me hurt you."

And to his wife, "Gretchen, call the police. This boy may have to go to the hospital."

After she'd made the call, Mrs. Stahel knelt beside me in the ditch. "I'm a nurse. Let me check you." I am certain she tried to be gentle, but it hurt wherever she touched.

The police arrived. When I gave my name, the officer asked, "You are Mr. Pietro Bonogura's son?"

I nodded. Dad was an accountant with the police.

The officer asked his partner to call my dad.

"Who did this to you, boy?"

I started to cry. "Please don't make me tell you, officer."

"We have to find out," the policeman said.

"He'll kill me next time."

The policeman nodded his head. "He didn't miss it by much this time."

He questioned Mr. Stahel who said, "I was working in the garden on the side of my house and saw this big, fat boy sitting on his bicycle. He seemed to be waiting for someone. When this young man pedaled down the street, the fat one smashed his bike into him and began to beat him. I did nothing for a few seconds, you know, boys fighting. Soon, I could see it was more serious."

He was describing the fight when another police car arrived. Dad opened the door and ran to me. "Dué, what happened to you?"

Mr. Stahel answered the question. "A fat kid with red hair tried to hurt your son."

Dad looked at me. "Joey." It was a statement, not a question.

"Let it go, Dad. Please."

He looked at me. "We will discuss it later."

Mrs. Stahel stood and introduced herself. "You could take him to the hospital, but I don't think it's necessary."

"We'll do whatever you say," Dad said.

"In Switzerland, my home country, I was a nurse. If it was my child, I would watch him. If he does not get sleepy and does not start any new bleeding, I would keep him home. If he falls asleep for no reason or spits or passes blood, take him to Charity Hospital right away."

"Thank you. Can you stand, son?" Dad reached for my hand.

I could, but it was not any fun.

"You live right down the block. We'll give you a ride to your house, Mr. Bonogura," the policeman offered.

"Give me your address and, if you like, I will pass your house this evening after choir practice," Mrs. Stahel said.

Dad thanked her and helped me into the police car. "What happened, Dué? What brought this on?" Dad was pretty intense.

"I played a joke and it backfired," I said.

"Looks more like an explosion, son. Tell me."

I did and when I came to the part about the washcloth, the policeman made eye contact in the rearview mirror. He was grinning. "Was it worth it, kid?"

I nodded. "Up until a little while ago, anyway."

Even Dad almost smiled, though his concern for my well-being must have checked the impulse.

They helped me into the house and into bed. Aunt Na-ne and Aunt Rose took command, yelling at the world in angry Italian. Dad returned to my room and asked my aunts to leave us alone for a minute. "Dué, I'm most concerned about this. Joey is big and strong. He could hurt you real bad."

I said nothing.

"Over the last several months, I've watched you and your friends deal with Joey. I hoped you could work it out among yourselves. Looks like I was wrong. No matter. It's over."

With that, he left the room.

"Dad," I called after him.

My aunts returned. I heard the front door slam. The next sounds were the tires of the police car peeling out, followed by the wail of the siren.

Yes, I know I was not allowed to sleep, but I dozed off—a nap.

As bad as things were before, they got worse when I woke up. I opened my eyes to see my dad, the policeman, and beside him, the scariest woman in the entire Ninth Ward: Joey's mom.

Imagine a cylinder: a Sicilian cylinder wearing one of those black sack-like "one size fits all" dresses Sicilian women wear to mourn a death in their family, among friends, or someone they may have met. And then there was the hair—like anyone could forget that orange color. It had to be dye. God would not create a color that ugly.

To make matters worse, she was in tears. My dad had made the crazy mother of the neighborhood psychopath cry.

There were but two options, death or escape. I went with option number two and closed my eyes to plan an escape. There was no way I could stay in the old neighborhood. My dad had brought the police to Joey's family. That made me a rat!

Through the mental fog in which I was hiding, I heard Dad suggest to Joey's mom that she look at me, felt him lift the sheet to show the bruises on my chest and legs.

"Your son did this to my son. You know it. I know it. The man who called the police knows it." He motioned with his index finger. "Follow me. My son should rest. We will talk on the porch."

Later, Dad explained what had happened. Working together, he and the policeman had convinced Joey's mom that Joey was on his way to prison—not "juvie," where he had been before, but real jail.

"We told her that Joey's age was close enough for him to be considered an adult, and his crime, which was described as 'attempted murder,' would put him in a place with some real bad criminals. I did not say we would drop the charges, but that I'd sit and wait. Joey behaves, he stays free. He touches you or any of your friends, and he goes to jail."

I did not think it would work, but I was hopeful.

The news of the beating had spread. Police sirens were big events in our peaceful neighborhood. Members of the tribe visited under the close supervision of Aunt Rose. Aunt Na-ne was absent, off no doubt preparing some Sicilian potion to make me well and for sure calling upon her favorite Sicilian saints to place a curse on Joey.

Shortly after the last of my friends left, Aunt Rose tapped on the door sill. She had never done that. Announce herself? No way. "Dué, you have a visitor." There was an interesting smile on her face. She was always so serious, but there was a smile, one that erased years.

I turned my head to see the door. From the way she was acting, I thought it might be Father Pete, the priest who worked with the altar boys. He was one awesome guy.

Cheryl. Oops. "Dué, what happened?" She stepped next to the bed, reached her hand to my face. She looked upset.

Brave guy attempts smile. Movement of facial muscles causes pain. "I was in a fight."

"A fight! It looks like you've been hit by a truck."

I managed a nod. "Yeah, but it's over now, nothing broken or anything.

"But why, what happened? What caused the fight?"

This was dangerous terrain. If she ever learned the details of the practical joke, she might think I was sort of crude. This would be big trouble. I would have to be careful. "Doesn't matter. It's over."

"Oh my God! You started it?"

I managed a very small shake of my head. Movement was not a fun thing. "Not exactly. He threw the first punch, first bicycle actually, but I had done something to make him mad."

She moved like a mother addressing a child who was not very bright. "Dué, that smart mouth of yours is going to cause problems for you."

I tried the smile again. "I agree."

"So, what caused the fight?"

"Cheryl, if we both live to be 50 years old and meet on a streetcar sometime, I might have the courage to tell you."

She smiled. I was off the hook. "Did you tell your friends about the party?"

"I told them we went over to your cousin's house. Said it was bigger than the motels on Gentilly Boulevard."

Her reply was to look at me. I hated that look. Didn't know what she wanted. "I told them there was a pond full of fish in the back yard.

"And?"

"And what?"

"Did they tease you?"

She was looking so sweet, but I sensed danger, the edge of the minefield.

"Cheryl, to be honest, since that new girl, Ashley, moved into the school, they have been too busy following her around to notice anything I do."

A word about Ashley might be helpful. Remember how I said we cared very little about seventh grade girls, but devoted a lot of time to looking at older girls? There is a female developmental process that seems to launch sometime in seventh grade but doesn't really get underway until eighth.

Ashley had been living overseas and going to school by correspondence. Her parents held her back to repeat seventh grade for the "total school" experience. I had no idea what that meant—I just knew that her clothes were very tight. My three pals were like Ashley's shadows.

Cheryl leaned over the bed. I thought she was going to kiss me. My eyes scanned the room for Aunt Rose. This could be a problem. She put her hand on my cheek, as she did when we kissed at the party. "Dué."

"Yes," I croaked through my now-parched throat.

"If you join your friends in the Ashley parade, these bruises will be minor." She stood, turned, and left the room.

As she left, I noticed something. A few of her straight lines were becoming curves.

That pleasant thought process was interrupted by the sound of my grandfather coming into the house. This was mom's dad. Pappy did not do anything quietly. I heard Aunt Rose introduce him to Cheryl. I missed whatever he said to her, but heard her giggle.

He entered the room. "Damn, boy, you got your ass kicked!"

I nodded.

"Your dad told me the whole story. Good thing that neighbor was there. You could have been hurt."

"Pappy, this is what I call hurt."

He laughed and turned the conversation to a project he and I were working on for the clubhouse. He placed a bag of cookies on the bed. "Grandma said these would make you get better."

He paused in the doorway. "Had a chance to meet your girl-friend, Dué. Kind of scrawny now, but I'll bet she fills out nice."

Pappy was something else!

Chapter 6

This is probably a good time to discuss my grandfather and our clubhouse. For such a famous city, New Orleans does not take up a lot of land. Here's an example. From where we lived in the Ninth Ward on the eastern edge of town, we were a 20-minute bike ride to the swamp.

A long time ago, when the L&N Railroad completed the line through the swamp, it left behind all sorts of neat stuff: lumber, sea shells for the road bed, and assorted tools. All of these treasures had been dumped on a man-made shell island at the end of a spur off the main line.

Mick and Fat Tony had discovered the littered island. Talk about a place with potential! Over the next couple of months, we nailed together scraps of lumber and tin, and eventually we came up with something that an observer with a good imagination could have called a hut. We called it our clubhouse.

There came a time when the work had progressed enough to warrant a real adventure: a sleep-over in our clubhouse. In those days, before parents were terrified of having some sicko hurt their kids, we enjoyed a lot of freedom. Even so, there was no way anybody was going to let a group of seventh grade boys sleep in the swamp.

Mick thought he could pull it off. He only had to wait for his dad to come home drunk one night and do the usual: start arguments and beat the crap out of anyone who disagreed with him. Mick had survived by disappearing. Fat Tony also had a shot. With so many people living in his house, there was a better than even chance that he could disappear for the night. Jimmy and I were screwed. With loving, involved families, there was no way we could craft an unnoticed departure.

The two cards left on the table were lies and deception, useful tools for a lot of guys, and I can't say I was always an exception. But, after we lost Mom, well, there was no way I could be dishonest with

29

my dad. Instead, I tried a plan that had worked for me in the past. I came clean. "Hey Dad, got a minute?"

He pushed aside a stack of accounting books, lifted a cup of coffee. "Sure, Dué. What's up?"

I told him about the place in the swamp, that we had built a hut. Dad gave me his sad smile. I knew that smile. It meant he was thinking of Mom.

"Right now, I can feel Conchetta, looking down on us."

That was Mom's name, Conchetta. How's that for Italian! "Why's that, Dad?"

"Because, Dué, all of your curiosity about nature, the swamp, fishing—all of that came from her."

This was something new. In all of the pictures I'd seen, she had been dressed like she was on her way to church or a dance. "So, Dad, where did she get this love of the outdoors?"

"From a man who misses her every bit as much as you and I do, Dué—your grandfather." He said this with the same sad smile.

At that time, I had no idea why it was there or what it meant, but I felt this lump thing in the back of my throat.

"Dué, we miss your mom something terrible, but we have each other. Pappy does not have that."

"What about Grandma?" I was confused.

Dad shook his head. "I think your grandma's life pretty much ended when that car hit your mom. I know all of her joy did. She's angry, angry at everyone for that, from God all the way down to Pappy."

Sometimes it took Dad a few minutes to get to where he was going with a story. I had learned to wait.

Dad smiled, a good one this time. "Dué, I would be willing to bet that your friends' parents would let you boys spend the night in the swamp if Pappy was with you."

Now there was an idea. Dad had a habit of coming up with solutions to lots of problems. I stopped talking, paused to consider. All of the guys knew Pappy. In fact, that's what most of them called him. I wouldn't mind going camping with Pappy, but I wasn't sure how the rest of the tribe would feel.

"There is something else to consider, Dué."

"What's that, Dad?"

"I have never seen your clubhouse, son." He nodded his head like he was thinking while he spoke. "I am sure it is probably well-built."

It was my turn to nod. "It only leaks when it rains real hard."

"Dué, did you know that Pappy built the house where he and Grandma live? He did the whole thing by himself. I'm of the opinion that there isn't much he can't fix or build."

There was the selling point to the tribe! Dad had insisted that I say nothing to Pappy until after the guys had voted.

"Dad, do you think he'll do it?"

Dad was not a touchy-feely kind of person, at least not to the extent that Mom had been. But this time he reached across the table and tussled my hair. "Dué, this is going to be the best present you will ever give him."

Although the vote to ask him to join was unanimous, I believe it was because there was no other option. Bring some adult along or forget the adventure.

Dad was right. Pappy tried to act cool, but I could tell he was excited about the project.

Dad had suggested a meeting take place at our house, sort of neutral territory. The members of the tribe were crowded around the kitchen table. Pappy walked in with a bag of jelly doughnuts still warm from baking. He raised a finger. "One rule. You want me to join you on this adventure, we got one rule."

We waited.

"Nobody leaves the campsite without first talking to me."

He locked eyes with me. "Agreed, Dué?"

I nodded.

"And you, Jimmy?"

Another nod.

Fat Tony beat him to the question. "No sir. I won't go nowhere without your permission."

Mick made a judgment error. He tried to out-stare Pappy. After a moment, he flashed his grin, and agreed to the rule.

31

"Okay, so tell me about this place."

We stumbled all over ourselves describing the clubhouse to Pappy. After a few minutes, he popped a question. "You guys have time to take a ride with an old man?"

We climbed into his Chevy and gave him directions to the place where the tracks crossed a gravel road.

We piled out of the car and pointed into the swamp.

Pappy shook his head. "That gray-white lump out there?"

"Yep, Pappy," I said. "The shells are piled pretty high."

He nodded. "I can't see your clubhouse from here. Wait. That brown thing to the left, near the big tree?"

Jimmy answered, "That's the roof."

Pappy retrieved a measuring tape, a pencil, and a notebook from the trunk and followed us down the main track.

"Many trains pass here?"

"No, sir," Fat Tony said. "I don't think there are more than a couple a day."

Pappy extended his hand to stop us. "If you guys are on this track and see a train, don't run along the tracks. Step down into the swamp till it passes." He shook his head. "Once I watched a kid try to run away from a train. He tripped on a cross-tie. Talk about a mess."

That muted the conversation for the rest of the half-mile walk along the main track to the spur. The mood picked up as we neared the island. We showed him everything we had accomplished, talked about our plans. Pappy listened to our ideas, jotted notes, took measurements, and offered improvements for us to consider.

"It's your place, boys, but with a little work, it can be awesome." He pointed across the swamp to the road where he had parked his car. "There aren't many secrets in life, but this is as close to a secret place as I think you'll ever find."

The next weekend was the big event! We rode our bikes. Pappy met us at the intersection. I don't think he could have fit another nail inside his car. Jimmy groaned at the prospect of numerous trips along the tracks to carry everything.

Pappy laughed, asked us to relax, and removed several pieces of lumber from the car. In less than 10 minutes, he had assembled what he called a sled. It sat on top of the tracks—a wood platform on runners that were coated with grease to make it easy to slide. We emptied the contents of the car onto the sled and took turns pulling it along the tracks. When we reached the end of the spur, we unloaded the sled except for the two canvas bags that held Pappy's tent and sleeping bag.

"I'll pitch my tent on the sled, keep me off the ground."

I suppose that was his way of letting us know he would not be on top of us every minute. We'd sleep in our hut, and he would be across the island on the sled.

Pappy, Jimmy, and I fixed the roof while the other guys dug a fire pit for cooking.

The next project was a latrine.

By the end of the first adventure, the place was much improved. Over the next several weeks, with Pappy's help, we had increased the size of the cabin and added window flaps to allow for a breeze.

Pappy talked us out of constructing a door. "Guys, if someone happens along when we aren't here and sees a locked door, they are going to break in to see what's inside. We leave the place completely empty and open, no door. What if some bum comes along and spends a night or two? Hell, if he doesn't break anything who cares?"

"But then we have to lug all of our stuff in and out each time," Fat Tony complained.

Pappy grinned. "Maybe not. I have another idea."

We dug a hole in the shells and buried a huge ice chest. Into the ice chest went our mosquito nets, bug spray, fire starter, candles—all the essentials. When we were finished, we closed the top and swept shells over it. Even knowing where it was, it was difficult to find.

Chapter 7

When Dad had left for work on the day after the fight, his orders had been for me to stay in the house and let my aunts spoil me. I happily complied.

The houses on our street were small and very close together. I believe that the building code specified that the house had to be three feet from the property line, which equaled a six-foot space between houses. This was in the days before air conditioning. Everyone kept the windows open to catch an occasional breeze and to allow the window fans to move the air through the house, creating a man-made breeze. In the winter there was some privacy, but in the summer with the windows open, well, you heard a lot.

Paula, the daughter of the couple next door, had what we called a sudden wedding. This was normally followed six to eight months later by the birth of a child. I think the polite way of putting it was "They ran away and got married."

Paula was a reserved young lady. Sort of cute, though she didn't command the afternoon crowds generated by Colleen. Her personality was just on the dull side of quiet, which served to set the stage for me almost killing Dad.

Aunt Rose and Aunt Na-ne loved Dad and me, would have died for either one of us, but this didn't change the fact that they were two of the world's worst cooks. I have to give Dad high points for smooth talking in that area. He asked them to let us prepare most of our evening meals so we could have time together. I was stuck with their lunches, but fried bologna or peanut butter sandwiches are pretty foolproof.

That night, Dad and I had cooked one of his favorite "creations." Sometimes we did recipe things, but the dishes we invented were a lot more fun. This one was sautéed onions and peppers mixed with ground meat and wild rice. Now and then we added andouille sausage that Dad would get from a butcher he knew in Mid-City.

We were already through Grace and into the meal when he got to the small talk.

"So, Dué, how was your day? Rose and Na-ne spoil you?"

I smiled. "A little—but, Dad, I need to talk to you about something else."

He placed a fork-full of food in his mouth.

"I think maybe we need to talk to one of your police friends."

"Joey!"

I shook my head. "No, sir. Not Joey. The neighbors—I mean Paula's new husband."

Dad gave me a puzzled look. "What happened, Dué?"

"Dad, I think he's hurting her."

"How so?" he asked, and then made the near-fatal error of putting another fork-full of food in his mouth.

"Her parents were both at work today, and I heard these screams from her room. 'Oh no! Oh my God!' Do you think he was beating her?"

Dad started to choke. His face got red—really, really red. He stood, leaned over, choked even more until whatever had gone down the wrong way righted itself.

But no sooner had he caught his breath than he started laughing uncontrollably. What a fate—to narrowly survive a choking attack only to laugh yourself to death. And if he had died, it would have been my fault!

Finally he managed to shake his head and compose himself enough to address my concerns. "I don't think he was hurting her, Dué. After dinner we'll go for a walk and have a little talk."

This was the second part of "The Talk."

The first part took place a few months earlier, when I got sent home from school.

Every Friday, the nuns made us go to Confession. That's right, it was not optional.

Our parish had two priests. Father Pete was about my dad's age. He was in charge of the altar boys, coached all of the school's athletic teams, and ran the Dad's Club. He was everybody's favorite priest. Father Joe was the pastor. I guess he was nice, but he was real old and could get kind of grumpy. Since Father Pete was on vacation that week, Sister Mary Peter marched half of us to the neighboring parish to ease the load on Father Joe.

In case any non-Catholics read this, I guess I need to explain Confession. In those days our world was divided into two camps—Catholics and non-Catholics.

I don't know what non-Catholics did about sin, but we went to Confession.

Imagine three closets in a row, one in the center and one on either side. The priest sat in the center one. On each side of the priest, at his eye level, there was a small sliding door on the common wall connecting the side closets.

While the priest had a chair in his closet, all you got was a kneeling pad. Under the pad was a switch that controlled tiny red and green lights above the entry to the side closets. When you knelt the light turned from green to red so people would know that side was occupied. Instead of doors, heavy drapes covered the entry. It was some dark in there while you waited your turn and pretended not to listen to the sins of the person on the other side.

And eventually, following a thunderous creak, your little door slid open. A heavy screen separated you from the priest, the presumption being that if you couldn't see more than the outline of the priest, he couldn't see more than the outline of you.

Before the priest could speak, I launched into the formula the nuns had beaten into our little brains. "Bless me Father, for I have sinned." The next part of the recital was to say how long it had been since your last confession and, finally, to start listing your sins. The general tendency was to open with the small ones, like not listening in class. Then, very casually and in a progressively quieter tenor, mention the murder, arson, adultery, or grand theft auto as a series of afterthoughts.

I had been pretty good that week. The most serious thing I had to confess was throwing rocks at the cat across the street.

His outline shifting closer to the screen, the priest whispered, "How many times did you touch yourself, boy?"

Seeking clarification, I repeated the question. "Touch myself?"

"Yes, boy. How often do you touch yourself?"

A word problem—I was really good at those. Let's see, when I first wake up, once before school, once at recess or lunch break, once after school, and right before bed for a total of five. A lie in Confession is a big sin, so for safety's sake I padded the number. "About six times a day, Father."

Through the shadow of the screen, I saw his hand go to his forehead. The volume on his voice went up. "Six times a day! This must stop!"

It was as if we were speaking different languages. "Stop?"

"Yes, boy. Immediately! Jesus does not like little boys to touch themselves!"

"But, Father, if I don't touch myself when I pee, how will I aim?"

He came out of his booth, reached into mine, grabbed me by the arm, and yanked me out of the confessional. I was sent home.

That night, Dad and I had "Talk Number One."

Chapter 8

For as long as I live, I will associate Saturday mornings with hot doughnuts. Jimmy's dad knew a guy who managed a nearby McKenzie's bakery. He had given us a job. Each Saturday, my tribe would sweep the floor in the bakery and run errands for the owner.

In return for those tasks, which never occupied more than an hour of our time, we were paid with fresh, delicious, wonderful, hot doughnuts and a glass of ice-cold homemade chocolate milk. Food addiction starts at an early age in the Crescent City.

I believe everyone was surprised to see me in the bakery. Guess they thought I'd be in bed for a few days. Word of my beating—couldn't call it a fight—had spread through the neighborhood.

We finished work and, as usual, carried our fresh-baked treasures to a bench in the back of the bakery.

Mick was the first to speak. "Dué, this crap has to stop. I think we should ambush Joey. If we all had our baseball bats and jumped him, we could kick his ass."

I tried to speak, but Fat Tony was louder. "Damn right."

I stood. "Hold on, guys. My dad had a better plan."

"Your dad?" They spoke as if in chorus.

I walked them through the night's events and visitors.

"Your dad brought Joey's mom to your house?" Jimmy was having trouble forming a mental picture.

"Don't know how he did it, but she was there."

Mick shook his head. "Man, you are dead. Joey tried to kill you, but getting his mom involved—he ain't gonna stop till it's done."

Jimmy and Fat Tony's silence implied agreement with Mick's statement.

"Let me finish, guys." I explained the whole jail discussion Dad had shared with me. "Joey messes with any of us and he goes to jail."

Fat Tony shook his head. "Not gonna work, Joey's been to juvie before."

"Wrong! This ain't juvie. The policeman said Joey goes to real jail this time."

"No shit!" Jimmy seemed impressed. "Real jail. Damn, that might make him think before he beats the shit out of you again."

Mick's grin appeared. "He'll still beat the crap out of you, but he'll think first."

That was not what I had hoped to hear.

The discussion continued. The choices were to ambush Joey, have me run away as I had first planned, or wait and see what happened.

While I did relish the thought of beating Joey with a bat, we'd be screwed when he recovered—unless, of course, we killed him. Our inability to reach a decision was a decision.

We would wait and see.

To pass the time between waiting and seeing, Mick suggested we go fishing.

During the walk from the bakery, we developed a supply list. With one shoulder bandaged from the broken collarbone, Fat Tony had difficulty riding his bike. He could do it, but it was touch and go. He was absolved from carrying any supplies, but since his family owned a grocery, he would provide cans of Vienna sausage, pork and beans, and peanut butter. Jimmy would get the bread and carry the food. Mick and I would carry water.

Dad was in the kitchen, papers spread all over the table and on two of the four chairs. He was hard at work at one of his second bookkeeping jobs. Mom had been in a coma for weeks after the accident and had left a bunch of hospital and doctor bills behind.

When I came in, Dad looked up, always with that grin. "Feeling okay today, Dué?"

I nodded. "A little sore, Dad. Do you mind if we go fishing?"

Dad did a great job of frying the fish we caught. He asked me to be sure to get home before dark. We rode our bikes to the edge of the swamp and chained them to a tree near the tracks. Mick tapped me on the shoulder. "So for three months, Joey has been pissing on a wash cloth and patting his pimple-face with it?"

I grinned around the cut in my lip. "Think so."

He winked. "For that I might forgive you for trying to see

39

Colleen naked."

Jimmy had read a book about one of the national parks. In Yosemite, bears were a real problem. Food at campsites lured them into close contact with humans. None of us had seen or heard of any bears in our swamp, but we liked the idea of hanging our food from a tree to keep it safe. Thanks to Joey's kicks and punches, I was not very nimble, and neither was Fat Tony. Our job was to fish while Mick and Jimmy worked at getting a line over the branch of a cypress tree and rigging a pouch from a piece of canvas to hoist our emergency food supplies to a safe height.

It was a warm day. Know what happens in the swamp on the first warm day after a cool snap? All those snakes that have been in various stages of hibernation come out and explore.

It was not like a horror movie, *The Revenge of the Moccasins* or anything like that. On our last few trips to the camp, we had maybe seen one or two each time.

I counted six water moccasins that morning. Snakes were how we maintained the camp.

Perhaps I should explain.

Fat Tony's family's grocery store was in a tough neighborhood next to one of the city housing projects. Mister Eli, an old black man in that neighborhood, did odd jobs for Fat Tony's dad.

Mister Eli's other gig was in the medical profession, sort of. He bought poisonous snakes, milked them of their venom, and sold the venom to Charity Hospital. The hospital used the venom to make the remedy for snakebites.

Mister Eli didn't keep the snakes for very long. He would milk them a couple of times and then kill them. It was cheaper and easier to buy fresh snakes from kids like us than to try to keep them around his house. He paid twenty-five cents a foot for cottonmouth moccasins and fifty cents a foot for diamond-back rattlers.

There was no scouting program in our neighborhood—something about a problem with the scoutmaster—but we had come upon some of the scouting instruction manuals. What a storehouse of information for kids! There was a detailed diagram on how to make a snake stick, basically a broom handle with two nails driven into the end to form a "v" with an optional loop on the end. We had experimented with the scout version and had made a few modifications.

In a weird kind of conservation—before there was real conservation—we used the money from our snake sales to buy things for the camp. (Well, mostly. Now and again we treated ourselves to the movies.)

Since I was the only member of our tribe who did not have nosey, prying sisters, I was the treasurer. I kept the money in an old Community Coffee can under my bed.

"Hey guys," I yelled from where I was fishing. "There are a lot of snakes moving around. Want to catch a few to sell?"

Mick loved messing with snakes. "Be there in a minute, Dué. We're almost done."

"Hold on," Fat Tony, who was not crazy about the snakes, said. "How much money is left in the can?"

"We're down to three bucks and change."

"Who's gonna bring them to Mister Eli?" With every word, Fat Tony further distanced himself from the snake operation.

"I'll carry the sack in my bike basket," Jimmy said. "Like I do every frickin' time."

Jimmy, who once had a newspaper route, had a huge basket on his bike.

"I'll tag along with Jimmy," Mick volunteered.

While none of us voiced any fear of Mister Eli's neighborhood, we never went alone. Jimmy carried the sack in the bike's basket, secured very well, I might add, and either Mick or I, or sometimes both of us, rode alongside.

Going there by bus involved two transfers. And the other riders tended not to be comfortable around a gunnysack that moved.

The first time we had brought snakes back from the swamp, a huge thunderstorm had prevented us from riding our bikes to Mister Eli. We had taken the bus and had sat near the back door. There was an old black man sitting about three rows from us.

He watched the sack. After a little while, he spoke. "What you boys got in dat sack?"

We gave him puzzled looks.

"Sack's moving. What you got there? Turtles?"

Mick grinned. "Yessir. We got turtles, snapping turtles." From then on, if anyone became interested in the sack, we'd say there were turtles in it.

Fat Tony took over the fishing duties while the rest of us searched for snakes. By the time we were ready to head home, we had a respectable catch of perch and green trout for dinner and four snakes to sell.

Chapter 9

The day had been so much fun we had forgotten why we had gone fishing.

Trouble met us a block from Jimmy's house. Joey was leaning against a tree. "Been looking for you little fruits. Where you been? Hiding?"

Evidently Mick had drawn some mental line in the sand. "We got nothing to hide from. You mess with us, you wake up in jail."

This was not going well. I stepped between them. "Fishing, Joey, we've been fishing."

He sneered at me. "You didn't get enough the other day? You want some more?"

"No."

"My mother beat the shit out of me." His fists were clenched.

"Joey, you don't want to go to jail." I was working hard.

"I ain't afraid of jail."

"Never said you were."

It got quiet—a positive sign.

He exhaled, looked at Mick's feet, and changed the subject. "What's in the sack?"

"Snapping turtles," Mick answered, reaching down for the sack. "Want them?"

"No!" I shouted. "Snakes, Joey. There are snakes in there."

He stepped back and gave me a furious look. "Don't mess with me again, you little shit."

"I ain't messing with you, Joey. We have snakes in the sack, cottonmouth moccasins."

"Bullshit. You little fruits ain't got the balls to catch no snakes." He snatched the sack, shook it, and turned it upside down.

All the while I was shouting. "No! Joey! No!"

As the snakes tumbled out, one hit Joey's leg right below the knee. He screamed and dropped the sack. The other snakes slithered away, but the one that had struck his leg stuck. It must have caught its fangs in the fabric of his jeans. That snake, the biggest of the bunch, was twisting and shaking, trying to get loose. Joey had fallen to the ground and was making futile attempts to grab the snake and pull it away.

We all screamed! That's not exactly correct. Fat Tony didn't scream. He took charge. He must have pushed his fear of snakes out of his mind because he snatched the gunnysack from the ground and used it like a glove. Its rough texture allowed him to grab the snake and yank it from Joey's leg.

Screaming and sobbing, Joey tried to get up.

Fat Tony pushed him to the ground and sat on his chest. "Stay still, Joey. We gotta stop the poison from spreading."

My tribe had studied the first aid section of the scout book and, in moments of boyhood bravado, had talked about how we would do it—save a pal's life after a snakebite.

Fat Tony had established leadership. We followed his directions.

"Jimmy, run to somebody's house and call the cops."

"Mick, you and Dué catch that snake and cut its head off. Joey should have it with him when he gets to the hospital so the docs will know it was a moccasin."

Mick pulled the machete from our swamp bag and went after the snake. In two steps he was on it, whacking it into little pieces.

"Guess we better get rid of the others too," I said.

The smaller snakes had a head start but suffered similar fates.

We returned to Joey and Fat Tony. Just like in the book, Fat Tony had used his belt to make a tourniquet above the bite. He threw his pocketknife in my direction. "Anthony, go over to that house and run this under the faucet."

Even Joey, who continued to cry, listened to Fat Tony. I cleaned the knife blade under the stream of water and returned it to Fat Tony. He remained on Joey's chest, effectively blocking Joey's view of his leg. Fat Tony had cut Joey's pants leg before he had tossed the knife to me to clean it.

Mick and I looked down at Joey's leg. The main puncture marks were clear, angry red slashes against the pale background of Joey's leg. There were other smaller scratches near it, probably from when the snake was trying to get loose.

We could see that the leg was changing color. We thought it was the poison taking hold, but learned this was evidence of the effectiveness of the tourniquet.

Fat Tony mouthed instructions to us so Joey would not hear what was about to happen. The orders were to hold Joey's arms. He was not going to like the next step in first aid.

Probably because his family owned a grocery store with a butcher shop, Fat Tony's knife was the sharpest one in the tribe. It was on a par with the barbershop razor.

He made a deep "X" over the main bite and attempted smaller cuts over the other scratches, while Joey cursed, punched, and fought to get free. Fat Tony turned to face him. His voice was loud but calm. "Joey. If you stay still till the cops come, you get to live. You run around and let the poison race through your body, you die. Your choice." Fat Tony pushed himself off Joey.

Joey looked at his leg. The cuts had done their job. He was bleeding, more blood than I had ever seen.

His eyes were the size of Mardi Gras doubloons. He looked at us, eyes darting from one to the other. "I'm going to kill you little fuckers."

Mick grinned and said, "Only if you don't die first."

That was when we heard the first siren.

Chapter 10

People are funny about snakes. Neither the motorcycle policeman nor the ambulance crew had wanted anything to do with the head of the dead snake. They wouldn't even touch it.

They had asked Mick to place it in the gunnysack, which they handled with a medical instrument that looked a lot like a pair of pliers.

After the ambulance left, the policeman asked for Joey's address to notify his mom. There was no way I was going anywhere near that lady.

After that day, none of the members of our tribe ever called our friend "Fat Tony." He became "Tony." We were too young to understand what the change meant. Kids our age saved respect for grown-ups.

The ambulance left. The police followed. We stood around for a few minutes, then drifted away. We had never parted like that before. There was always a "see you later" or "anybody want to check out the playground?" Both the mood and our voices were muted somehow.

I got on my bike and pedaled off, no destination in mind. I think I may have been going in the general direction of Grandma and Pappy's, but that wasn't where I ended up.

There was a large magnolia tree in the lot across the street from Cheryl's house. Cheryl's dad had turned the driveway into a basketball half court. I sat on my bike, leaned against the tree and watched her play.

She practiced every day that it didn't rain. It was a pleasure to watch her. She shot free throws, always sets of 10, drove to the basket for lay-ups, and nailed every shot from the corner. From the way she twisted, turned, faked, and moved, you could tell she was pretending she was in a game with another player guarding her.

Finally she glanced in my direction, and her practice stopped. Squinting—because her distance vision was not that good—she dribbled the ball down her driveway.

"Dué?"

I waved. "Hi."

"What are you doing over there?"

I walked the bike toward her. "Watching you practice."

"That's weird." But she said so with a smile. "You don't look any better. How do you feel?"

"From the fight—I'm recovering. But there's some other stuff going on." Even as I said this, I wasn't sure what, exactly, I wanted to say or how I knew that Cheryl was the person I wanted to say it to.

Mrs. Wolf stepped out of the side door and onto the drive. "Cheryl Ann?"

"Yes, Mom, Dué's here."

She motioned to us. "Come here, Dué. I want to have a look at you."

I got inspected frequently during the days after the fight—or massacre, to use Jimmy's most recent description.

Mrs. Wolf said the "oh" and "my goodness"—the typical stuff—over my appearance. "What started the fight?"

I shook my head. "Can't really say."

At her mother's direction, Cheryl poured two glasses of water, and we walked out to the big glider swing in her back yard.

Cheryl whispered, "You know I'm going to find out."

I played dumb, an increasingly easy task in her presence. "Find out what?"

"I'm going to find out what started that fight."

I offered a grin. "Like I said when you came to the house, when we're 50 years old, look me up in the phone book and I'll tell you."

She gave me the strangest look—wish someone would write a book or teach a course to help guys decipher things like that.

We sipped the water in silence.

"You think if you stay here long enough, Mom will bring out cookies?"

I stood. "I'm sorry, Cheryl. Guess I should be going."

She grabbed my hand and pulled. "Sit down, Dué. I was joking.

There's something wrong. What happened?"

So much for the strong, silent type. I spilled my guts—the club-house, the snakes, how we sold them and used the money, and, finally, the snakebite. I did manage to preserve one secret: our location in the swamp.

"Let me see if I understand this. You and that gang of fools have been catching poisonous snakes and carrying them on your bikes?"

Her face had been a little flushed from the basketball workout—now it was bright red. Even then, I was glad I'd told her the story. I had no idea why doing so made me feel better. For the moment, the more important question was why girls got so much cuter when they were mad.

I offered a feeble defense of the tribe's logic. "Cheryl, we're not stupid. We had them in a sack."

"But, what if one of you had been bitten while you were at your stupid clubhouse? You could have died!"

"Cheryl, all of that's over. No more snake hunting, I promise. Heck, when my dad gets wind of this, he may even forbid me from ever going to the swamp again."

"There is that hope." She took my hand and turned to face me, and then she did the strangest thing with her eyes—it was as if she were looking through her lashes. Until that moment I'd thought eyelashes were like shutters on windows. Just something to keep the dust out.

In the softest of voices, she asked, "Dué, does anybody call you by your real name?"

"You mean 'Anthony'?"

She nodded, still holding my hand and doing the eyelash thing.

I paused in thought. "No, I don't think so."

"Would it be all right with you if, when we're alone, at special times like this, I called you Anthony?"

I was having voice problems. "That would be real nice," I croaked.

And there we stayed, holding hands, looking at each other.

Eventually, though, the time came to head home and face Dad.

"Cheryl," I said, "you can't tell anybody about this stuff."

She reached across the table and touched my arm. "You're my friend. Anthony." As she said my name she put the lashes back in action. "And friends respect confidences. If Mom and Dad ask, I'll have to tell them, but they'll keep it to themselves."

She allowed me to walk a few steps toward my bike.

"Anthony."

I turned. "Yes?"

"Did you forget anything?"

God, I hate pop quizzes. I checked my pockets. "I don't think so."

She shook her head like I was slow or something and pointed at the street. "Go."

I was confused, but she seemed to have that effect on me.

A thought came to me one the ride home. If I was cool like the guys in the movies, I would have handled the special name thing in a different manner.

"Sweetie, if you look at me like that, you can call me po-boy sandwich if you want."

Chapter 11

It was Saturday—dawn of the worst day of the worst week of my life. In fact, when dawn broke, the day was, for me, already underway.

I had retrieved my bike from the shed in our back yard and had pushed it down the narrow alley between our house and Paula's. Ever since Dad had told me what those sounds meant, I paid special attention whenever I passed Paula's bedroom window. It was cool and clear out, a beautiful day in the making.

I was scheduled to serve at the "Fisherman's Mass," a poorly attended service Father Pete held each week to offer anglers the opportunity to attend Mass before heading out to Lake Pontchartrain.

There was a bike rack next to the rear door of the church. I placed my bike in a slot and secured it with a chain and a padlock. The sacristy door was locked. I walked across the asphalt-covered schoolyard to the convent.

The procedure was for the altar boy—there were no altar girls back then—to check the screen door to the convent. If the Sister scheduled to open the church wanted the altar boy to get started, there would be a key on the inner ledge of the screen door.

A smile crossed my face when I felt the key. Sister Mary Mercy had the duty. There was a note on the key. "Start the heater and light the candles, Dué. I'll see you in a few minutes."

Sister Mary Mercy deserves a few words. All of the nuns at our school, St. James Major, a.k.a. St. Jimmy the Great, were old. I mean really old. Sister Mary Mercy was in her first year of teaching. I can't imagine she was older than 25. Young—full of life, hope, and laughter. I can't say she was truly beautiful. I had no way of knowing—the habit the nuns wore covered much of her face and all of her hair.

Beauty, in her case, was beside the point. She was awesome! She played basketball with her class and was deadly on outside shots.

When she and Cheryl went one on one on the basketball court, people stopped to watch the game.

They didn't keep score. Two men would definitely have kept score. There was probably some lesson for us in that. I continue to work on it.

I ran over to the sacristy door, opened it, and walked to the heating control panel located down the hall and next to the room where we changed into our cassocks and surplices.

Not a Catholic? The cassock is a long, black robe that buttons down the front. The surplice is a sort of white shirt worn over the cassock. We were allowed to wear the surplice only during the actual Mass. This rule was based upon economics, not theology. Limited exposure cut down on spills and laundry bills.

After I moved the heater switch to the "on" position, I stepped into the change room and put my cassock on over my clothes. In the hall, on my way back to the sacristy proper, I flipped the switch marked "Daily" to turn on a limited number of lights in the church.

Sister Mary Peter had driven the electricians to tears over those switches. There was one for daily Mass, one for Sunday, another for daytime weddings, and a fourth for evening weddings. It was her way of making sure that none of Jesus' money was wasted on unnecessary utility bills.

In the main part of the sacristy, where the priests donned their vestments, I opened the wine closet using the same key I had used on the sacristy door. It was quite an honor to be trusted with that key.

The big blower for the heater had been put on a delay timer. It kicked in with the force of a gust of wind as I poured wine into a cruet, a small glass bottle that resembles a restaurant salad dressing container.

Several minutes later, a creaking noise disturbed the stillness of the church. It reminded me of the sounds of big mooring lines on riverboats and barges as they struggle with the swirling currents of the Mississippi River. It was rhythmic, back and forth, back and forth.

More curious than afraid, I looked around. Something in the

shadows across the room was moving. Whatever it was, it was above the floor.

I don't want to sound brave, but an empty church had never been spooky for me, probably because I had spent so much time in church praying for Mom. Somehow I had gotten the idea that if she didn't recover from the accident, it was because I hadn't prayed enough.

Sister Mary Mercy had gotten me off that guilt trip. "Dué, don't pray for your mother. Jesus will take care of her. Pray that you will let Jesus come into your heart to help you and your father."

All that aside, I have to admit I was thinking about ghosts as I strained my eyes to adjust to the darkness. Something was suspended from the ceiling. I walked across the room.

I never saw his face, and I thank God for that.

I identified the body as Father Pete's by his shoes. He was the only priest I had ever seen who wore black, umpire-like tennis shoes. He said he wanted to be ever-ready to take a jump shot or go out for a long pass.

I didn't scream and I didn't cry. I turned and ran like a sprinter in an Olympic-qualifying heat. In an incredible coincidence of timing, I arrived at the sacristy door at the precise moment Sister Mary Mercy opened it. I took her down like a linebacker on a wide receiver.

For a brief moment I was stunned, pan-caked on top of the nun, totally out of it. The points of Sister Mary John's shoes brought me back to reality. She was kicking me. "Get up, you filthy young man! Get off of her!"

Collecting what remained of my wits, I rolled off Sister Mary Mercy, but this did little to curtail Sister Mary John's assault.

I stood, ignored my attacker, leaned over and reached for Sister Mary Mercy's hand. "I am so sorry, Sister." I cried. "Father Pete—"

Sister Mary John stopped kicking. "Father Pete? There is something wrong with the priest?"

Through my tears I tried to explain what I had seen.

Sister Mary John ran through the open doorway.

Sister Mary Mercy, meanwhile, managed to sit up. When she

caught her breath, she asked what was the matter with Father Pete.

It was hard to say the words. Maybe if I didn't say them, what I'd seen wouldn't be real. "He's hanging in the sacristy, Sister."

Her hand went to her mouth. She forced herself to her feet and followed Sister Mary John into the church.

I stayed in the yard. The first wave of nausea hit. I was on my knees, leaning against the wall, taking deep breaths when Sister Mary John returned. She must have thought I was praying.

"Pray for his family, young man. Pray for his family."

I turned to face her. "I'll pray for Father Pete."

"It's too late to pray for him. There is no forgiveness for the sin of suicide. He's in hell."

When the nausea passed, I returned to the church to check on Sister Mary Mercy. She was on her knees, rosary in hand.

Chapter 12

Within minutes, two uniformed officers arrived and secured the entire church with yellow crime-scene tape. The detective assigned to the case arrived a little later. He had picked up my dad on the way to church.

Detective Perry secured the area, spoke briefly with the nuns, then turned his attention to me. "Sister says you were first on the scene. Tell me what you saw and felt. I want to hear everything."

He listened, made notes in a small notebook, and said nothing until I finished.

"That's it?"

I lowered my head. "When I left the sacristy, I was running. I met Sister Mary Mercy at the door and knocked her down."

He smiled. "From the way Sister described the hit, I guess you could play football for Tulane." And just like that, he became serious again. "Anything else?"

"No sir," I said. "Except that I went back in for a minute."

"Why?"

"I wanted to check and make sure Sister Mary Mercy was okay. Me knocking her down and all."

"Makes sense. How was she?"

"She was on her knees praying her rosary. It was kind of a weird picture. Sister Mary Mercy on her knees praying, while Father Pete's body hung above her head."

Suddenly he stopped writing. "Above—" He turned toward the church. "Stay here, boy."

Though puzzled, I knew better than to ask questions. He was back in minutes and motioned for me and Dad to follow him to the convent. He knocked on the door and waited for one of the nuns to open it.

"Sister, may I use your phone? The news people monitor the police radio."

Sister Mary John indicated a phone in the parlor.

He picked up the phone, dialed a number. "Lieutenant, we have a homicide on our hands."

The detective didn't curse, but his Lieutenant sure did—words I'd bet had never been heard on the convent phone.

"Sir, I had another look at the scene, and I think the priest's body was hanging too high for him to have jumped off the chair."

When the Lieutenant finished yelling, the detective placed the phone in its cradle. "Kid, you did real good. There is one other thing I want from you." He handed a business card to me. "Somebody killed your priest. If you remember anything out of the ordinary, anybody acting weird around the church, call me."

I looked at Dad. "Think it's important?"

"Tell him, son. Everything is important in a murder investigation."

I told him there had been a "creepy guy," a man who had interrupted my altar preparations before Mass one morning last week.

"From the top, the whole story." He let out a deep breath, almost a sigh, and sat back in his chair. "There is no hurry, Dué. Take your time. Don't leave anything out."

I spent a few minutes trying to decide where I should begin. "My job before Mass was to get the altar ready for the priest. The first thing I did was carry the cruets of wine and water to the table by the wall." I looked to Dad for reassurance. "After that, I walked behind the altar to get the matches to light the candles. When I was lighting the first candle, I kind of felt someone coming." I paused, looking for a way to express the sensation.

"I don't remember him making any noise—somehow I just knew someone was moving toward me. I turned and watched him step over the altar rail. Nobody's allowed on that side of the rail except for the priests and altar boys."

"That's right," the detective said. "I used to be an altar boy."

"I walked over to the man and spoke in a very low voice so I wouldn't disturb the others in church. I told him he shouldn't be on the altar, it wasn't allowed. He grabbed my arm. He was strong and squeezed it hard, said something about wanting to see the priest after Mass. I told him what the regular Confession schedule was, but that wasn't good enough. He squeezed my arm harder and hissed, 'You tell that fucking priest he'd better get out here.'

"I told Father Pete about it—all except the F-bomb. Father didn't say a word. We went out on the altar for Mass as if nothing had happened. And when Mass was over, Father went into the Confessional booth—as if it were the normal time for Confession—and waited for the creepy guy."

Chapter 13

Police business occupied the remainder of my day. Detective Perry had asked one of the uniformed officers to drive us to headquarters. Dad had made sure I was comfortable with the sketch artist before he went to his office. When the artist, who was really cool, had created a reasonable likeness, he turned me over to a lady who showed me a zillion pictures of criminals. "And all of these people did bad things?" I asked.

"Young man, we have rooms full of these books."

Dad and I rode home together on the bus. Aunt Na-ne had fixed a stewed chicken that was mighty good. We made a point of complimenting her.

The events of the day had wiped me out. I hit the sack early that evening. From lights-out until midnight, the moment of sin, I slept a deep, dreamless sleep. Sister Mary Mercy awakened me. She was not in the room, but the memory was. The moment of impact! For the briefest of moments, I had been on top of her, had felt her body pressed to mine. The memory of that moment was not a sin. It was a temptation. Not chasing the memory away, rejoicing in the feelings it triggered—big time sin!

Sleep was an elusive target. Dawn delivered knowledge of the gravity of the sin, a sin that could not be forgiven because it could not be confessed. How could anyone, even in the presumed anonymity of the Confessional, admit to having and, more importantly, relishing those sorts of thoughts about a nun. We were taught to think of the sisters as brides of Christ.

The next question was how to keep the world from knowing that Dué, committer of a mortal sin, was destined for hell?

I would resign from the altar boys. If an altar boy did not receive Communion, the priest would want a reason. Heck, anybody in church would wonder. "An altar boy not receiving communion, what had he done?"

If Cheryl ever noticed it, there would have been more questions

I could not answer.

I would use Father Pete's death as an excuse, say I was afraid of the sacristy. Good, another sin added to the total, a lie. But with a mortal sin on the books, lies would not even register.

Dad interrupted my half-sleep. "Dué, time to get up."

He usually let me sleep in when there was no school, but this was my busy day. Even with all of yesterday's events, I had chores. The morning was set aside to help Aunt Rose and Aunt Na-ne with odd jobs around the house: cut the grass, weed the gardens, empty some trash from the back shed.

I was supposed to tutor Cheryl after lunch, but Mrs. Wolf had said that if I finished my jobs in time, I could have lunch with them.

Aunt Rose commented on how quickly I tended to their list. The motivation was as much for the meal as it was to see Cheryl. Her mom was an awesome cook and the promised lunch was homemade German sausage—talk about good!

One strange thing happened on the bike ride over there. A few houses before I reached her house, I heard a car behind me. It sounded as if it were speeding. I turned into a driveway to get on the sidewalk, out if its way. It wasn't all that close, but something about it didn't feel right.

As it passed, I saw it was a Hudson Hornet.

We talked a lot about Father Pete during lunch and said some special prayers for him. It seemed to me that while all of us were saddened, we were also confused as to why anyone would want to hurt such a fine man. Mrs. Wolf wanted to know if the police had been nice to me. I told her they had been great.

Cheryl cleared the kitchen table after lunch and set places for us to study. We were working on a math puzzle when her mother stepped into the kitchen. "Your grandma will be here in a few minutes. I have to go to the grocery."

Cheryl said, "Mom, remember Daddy wanted some pretzels."

"Already on my list," she said as she stepped out the door.

Her grandmother lived next door. There is a lot of that in New Orleans, families living close together. Cheryl made the introductions, and the elder Mrs. Wolf walked to the living room with a crossword puzzle in hand.

We finished our math puzzle and checked the work.

"Anthony," she said when we were alone, "can I ask you something?"

Clueless reply numero uno: "Sure."

"Am I your first girlfriend?"

My head spun around twice. "Cheryl. Your grandma's in the other room."

Coy smile. "Granny's mostly deaf, Anthony."

I nodded, not to answer "yes" to the girlfriend thing, but to convey that I understood about Granny.

"Well?" She did the eyelash move again.

Last week's answer, before I learned what little I knew about navigating the minefield, would have been something like, "Holy cow, Cheryl. We have been going to school together since kindergarten. Have you ever seen me hanging around any other girls?"

Now, I was smoother. "I have never been friends with a girl before, Cheryl." I glanced into the living room to check on Granny, offered my best grin and said, "Never kissed one either."

That earned a high-beam smile. *Damn, I was good.*

"I was glad you came to talk to me about what happened in the swamp and even happier that you can talk to me about Father Pete. That is what real friends do, you know. Real friends share everything."

There was no need to ruin her day. Everything wasn't happening, not even close.

"Remember, the other day I asked if you had forgotten anything?"

"Yeah. Bad manners, forgot to thank your mom for letting me visit."

If Granny did not hear Cheryl's sigh, she totally deaf. "Anthony, you still don't know what it was?"

I shook my head.

Cheryl had set our books next to each other at the kitchen table. Our chairs were a couple of inches apart. Well, all of a sudden her leg touched mine—a real soft touch, but one that had a huge effect on me. My pulse rate doubled!

She whispered, "A kiss would have been nice."

I did the head spin thing again to check on Granny. "Cheryl, your mom was in the kitchen."

She smiled. "And we were outside. Besides, Mother likes you."

My life had become more difficult and complex. While I cannot say I did not enjoy the feelings I was experiencing with her, fishing with the guys was a whole lot simpler existence.

When I did not say anything, she winked and continued. "I have an idea."

Girls must read books about this or something. Maybe I could go to a library and find those books, not feel and act so dumb. I guess I smiled. "What's that?"

"Just suppose we were someplace where we wanted to kiss, but couldn't."

"Lots of places like that," I replied.

"We could have a secret sign, a substitute for a kiss."

I nodded as if I understood. "Sure, like fishing with a plastic lure instead of live bait." *Victory! I had finally confused her.* But she was smarter than I. Instead of trying to decipher something she did not understand, she dismissed it.

"Make a fist, Anthony."

"Which hand?" I wanted to get this right, whatever it was.

She shook her head. "It doesn't matter."

My right hand formed a fist and I extended it in her direction. She also made a fist. I paused to marvel at how a hand so tiny could perform such magic with a basketball. Her fist approached mine and her knuckles, with a touch so light I hardly felt it, brushed against mine.

She performed the smile and eyelash thing and asked, "Nice?"

Had I been a dog, I would have bayed at the moon. "Oh yeah, that'll work."

I would never have thought that touching a girl's knuckles with mine could have generated such feelings. Thank God her mom came home. I would have probably kissed her right there in the kitchen.

Mrs. Wolf placed the grocery bags on the table. I said it was time for me to head home. As I walked out the door, Cheryl whispered my name.

I turned toward her. We did the knuckle brush thing. Life was good.

Chapter 14

What happened next was not her fault. Even if I had not been distracted with thoughts about her, I don't believe I would have noticed in time. As I turned on to my street, Lavender Street to be precise, I heard the sound of squealing tires and an accelerating engine. I glanced over my shoulder. The Hudson Hornet was headed for me, its distinctive hood ornament aimed at my chest. As it passed, I caught a glimpse of the driver, the creepy guy from church.

I almost made it to the ditch. The car's left fender clipped my rear tire and sent me spinning across Mister DeRocca's lawn. The next sound was that of tires skidding on the street as the Hudson came to a stop and reversed direction. The noise masked the pop of the pistol, but I did feel wood splinters hit my back as I dove under the house. Neighbors came out of their doors, yelling and pointing at the speeding car.

The houses on my street were all pier and beam construction, raised a couple of feet above the ground. This little Italian scrambled under the houses moving from one to the other until I reached the alley by the grocery store three doors from my house. I checked the street for any sign of the car and raced inside. "Mister Luna, I gotta use your phone."

"Dué, what's amatta," he said in his broken English.

"My dad, I have to call him."

Dad sounded as out of breath as I. "Son, are you all right? Aunt Rose called. A car knocked some kid off a bike. She said there was gunfire!"

"It was me, Dad. I am really scared." Tears were not far away.

"Where are you?"

"At Mister Luna's store."

"Stay there. A car has already been dispatched to our street. Do not leave the store until a police officer comes in and asks for you by name. Put Mister Luna on the phone."

I don't know what Dad said. The conversation was in rapid

Italian. All I heard on my end was Mister Luna saying, "Si, si."

Before they finished the conversation, and as the store owner nudged me toward the back room, I heard the police siren. Minutes later, Officer Dooley walked into the store, introduced himself to Mister Luna. He called my name. "Dué, Dué Bonogura, your dad sent me to get you."

I walked to the counter, rubbed my sleeve across my eyes. I did not want the cop to see my tears.

He made a playful punch at my shoulder. "It's going to be all right, pal. We'll catch the guy. Come on."

We walked down the store's side alley toward our street. Officer Dooley said Dad had asked him to make a stop at our house, have me pack a bag, and bring me to the station. "Can I get my bike first?"

He nodded. "Sure."

When we emerged from the alley onto Lavender, the street was packed. The commotion had emptied the houses. People were touching me. "You all right, Dué?"

The bruises Joey had left had not yet faded, and here I was bunged-up again. Guess who was waiting by my bike? Cheryl.

No knuckle touch and I guess she did not care who saw us. She hugged me. "Dué, as soon as you left I heard a car race down the street, then the noise, the siren. Mom drove me here."

I looked at Mrs. Wolf, nodded my thanks.

"Cheryl, I'm fine. Dad asked Officer Dooley to stay with me while I packed some clothes. They are going to keep me somewhere safe until they catch this guy."

"Will you call so I'll know you're all right?"

"If there's a phone, I will." I had a thought. "Tell you what. If you don't hear from me, go see Aunt Rose. She'll know what's happening."

Officer Dooley lifted my bike. "Come on, Dué. We have to go."

I looked at Cheryl, made a fist. We did the thing. It worked. She smiled.

Aunt Rose met us at the door, fussing over me as usual. Aunt Na-ne is the most Sicilian woman in the family. She wrote Officer

Dooley's name and badge number on a pad. "Anything happens to my boy, I'm gonna find you."

He laughed, but it was forced. I think he believed her.

Dad met us at the door of the police station and greeted me with a hug. He carried my bag to his office.

I don't know why, but I almost cried. I was glad I didn't. It was important to me that Dad think I was brave.

The morning paper, the *Times-Picayune,* was on his desk. "Here is what caused your problem, son."

The headline was huge. "Altar Boy to Finger Priest Killer."

I said nothing—looked to my dad for advice.

"Somebody must have talked to the news people. Your name was not mentioned, but we can see it did not take the killer long to find you."

I told him I should have realized something on the first attempt to run over me.

"Son, you are a boy, a seventh-grade school kid. There was no way you could have suspected that anyone was after you."

"So, what are we going to do? Where are you going to hide me 'til they catch him?"

I was not expecting a smile, but when I saw one, it made me feel better.

"Pappy and I have had a couple of phone conversations. My first thought was to have you stay with them. Pappy was concerned about that. He did not know how Grandma would deal with the knowledge that you were in danger. He proposed an alternate plan. He thought he'd tell Grandma that the two of you were going to go fish at that clubhouse in the swamp for a few days."

It was my turn to smile. "Cool."

"I knew you'd like that." He paused. "Pappy will be here as soon as he gets everything ready for your adventure. You can hang out with me 'til then."

"Dad?"

"Yes?"

"Don't want to sound like a wimp, but do you think we'll be safe out there? It's really isolated."

He could have said that if he did not think it was safe he would not have allowed it, but that's not how Dad did things. He took the time to explain. "First of all, only you, Pappy, and your friends know the place exists." He laughed. "Heck, I don't think I could find it. And most importantly, anyone who wants to hurt you has to go through Pappy. I don't think I would like to try that." Dad paused as if he were thinking. "Dué, here is something you should know about your grandfather. It might make you feel a little better about this arrangement. When your mom was a little girl, our country was in what was called 'The Great Depression.' Pappy had to go overseas to find work. He was hired as a bodyguard for a very rich man in Honduras." Dad nodded. "He knows a lot about this sort of thing. You listen to Pappy and you will be fine."

Wow, that was something to think about. I had known Pappy was different from the other kids' grandfathers, but this made him super cool. I had stuffed one of those math puzzle books in my bag, but it couldn't hold my attention.

"Dad, can I use the phone?" I pointed to one on the empty desk across the room.

"Sure, but don't ever tell anyone about Pappy's other life."

"No way, Dad, that's our secret. Cheryl had asked me to call so she would know I was okay. I want to tell her that Pappy and I will be camping out, and I won't be able to call."

"Dué?"

"Sir?"

"Anything I should know about that?"

I hoped he did not notice my blush. "She's just nice, Dad."

He laughed. "That's how it starts, my boy. That is how it all starts."

Chapter 15

The phone on Dad's desk rang. The motor pool officer called to let Dad know Pappy was in the garage.

Dad picked up my bag. "Let's go. This is what I meant, Dué. Pappy knows things. I would have parked in front of the building. Pappy pulled into the garage so no one would see you get into his car."

Dad handed my bag to Pappy, turned, and hugged me.

Pappy said, "Dué, get in the back seat and lie down. We don't want to have bad luck and pull up next to this criminal at a stop light and have him see you."

He looked at Dad. "Get these guys you work with on a stick to catch this son of a bitch. Our boy will be fine with me. And when you catch him and come to tell us, make sure you or whoever you send comes in the daytime and makes a lot of noise. Anybody who sneaks up on us is going to get hurt."

Dad said, "I was counting on that."

As we pulled out of the police garage, Pappy gave me my first psychology lesson.

"Boy, I'm proud of you. You've been a very brave guy. What with your description and one of your neighbors' getting the license plate number, the cops should catch him pretty quick. I only know of one thing you've done wrong."

"What's that, Pappy?"

"This name you call him, 'the creepy guy.' That's not a good thing. While you may not realize it, when you say that, you're giving him power over you."

I did not understand and said so.

"The words 'creepy guy' are scary. Without knowing it, you're making yourself afraid of him. You need to find something else to call him."

I thought about that.

"Let me help. What color is his hair?"

"Kind of brown," I said.

"We could call him 'Brownie,' a name like you'd give to a dog."

"Brownie," I said the word, but felt no better.

"There's another option." I watched him adjust the rearview mirror so he could see me. "I know your Dad doesn't curse, and he doesn't like bad language, but while we're together in the swamp, how about we refer to the killer as 'asshole'?"

I laughed.

"Don't try to tell me you have never said anything like that, Dué. I've heard you and your friends on our campouts."

"We didn't think you could hear us."

"Well, I could." He grinned in the mirror.

"So, I can say it? You won't be mad?"

"Try it, boy."

"He's an asshole," I said.

"Louder," Pappy ordered.

"Asshole!"

"Louder!"

I shouted. "The creepy guy is an asshole!"

Our laughter carried us to the edge of the swamp. Pappy unloaded the car. I jogged alongside the tracks to our island and retrieved the sled.

I arranged the supplies on the sled and waited for Pappy to return. He had driven to a junkyard a mile or so down Gentilly Highway. Whenever we camped out, Pappy paid the owner a few dollars to leave his car there so it would not be sitting by the side of the road, an easy target for theft.

"I don't think we'll be out here too long, but I brought some stuff to work on a few projects to help pass the time."

"Sure, Pappy. What's first?"

"We'll make preparations so we don't have to think about the asshole." He stopped the sled a few feet after we had turned off the main line onto the spur. He opened one of the bags. "To keep anybody from sneaking up on us, we'll set a few alarms."

The bag he had opened was full of empty tin cans. Using his pocketknife, he punched holes in the cans and ran monofilament fishing line through the holes. He spread the line across the tracks. "The rocks on either side of the tracks are too steep to walk comfortably. Anybody who comes out here will walk the tracks and I promise you they will trip over one of our alarms."

Dad was right, Pappy knew things.

He clapped his hands together. "Time to develop a plan. Follow me."

Pappy built and sold pirogues to supplement his pension. A canoe with a flat bottom—that's your basic pirogue. Pappy had given us one for the camp. The water was not deep, but a pirogue could float on a damp sponge. The swamp bottom was muck. It was easy to sink up to your waist.

I followed him to the place where we hid the pirogue and it was there that he did one of the most awesome things ever. "Let's talk about a plan, Dué. First, what's the goal?"

"To keep me safe from the asshole." I was starting to like that word. Pappy had been right. Maybe I was still scared of the guy, but not like before. The awesome thing was that over the next few minutes, Pappy and I worked together on a plan. I'm sure it was the plan he wanted all along, but he made me feel a part of it. Pappy believed that the simpler the plan, the greater the chance of success. If we heard the cans rattle, we'd stop whatever we were doing and meet at the pirogue. Pappy had sketched a map in the mud with his knife.

The main road was about a mile south of our island. We'd paddle there and separate. Pappy would circle back to disable the asshole's car. My job was to run in the other direction to the post office. There was a pay phone on the outside wall of the building. I was to use that to call the operator and have her call the police. Pappy would follow the asshole so he could lead the police to him.

I remember asking Pappy what would happen if the asshole saw him.

"That would be his bad luck, boy."

I looked at Pappy and believed him.

"Now, let's forget about all that crap and work on our camp."

On the tribe's last outing, we had discussed building an observation deck in a tree. Pappy had explained that if we studied the water, we would be able to see minnows swimming near the surface. "You see minnows or bugs, maybe not right away, but sooner or later, there will be fish."

The tree we selected was a giant Louisiana Red Cypress on the edge of the shell island. Pappy and I passed the afternoon building a ladder up the side of the tree. When I reached a "v" about twenty feet above the ground, Pappy climbed up to study it with me.

He had carried a length of rope with him. He took some measurements, climbed down and cut a few boards: 2x4's for the frame and 1x6's for the deck. He used the rope to hoist them up to me.

With Pappy calling the shots, we completed the job a lot quicker than I had expected. We had a place like the crow's nest on a ship. Talk about cool! Two of us could sit up there and check the water surface for bait. We could also see the whole length of the railroad tracks.

Pappy made the climb and sat there with me. We studied the water surface. It was flat and still.

Pappy pulled a pipe from one of the many pockets in what he called his "camping" vest and began the ritual of filling the bowl with tobacco, tamping it to the desired density, and lighting his pipe. From experience I knew this was the prelude to one of Pappy's stories. I shifted into a comfortable position.

"Dué, that beating you took has been bothering me."

This would have been a good time to let him know that the combination of Dad's conversation with Joey's mom and Joey's getting bitten by the snake seemed to have ended that problem, but Pappy did not like interruptions.

"Your father is truly a gentle man. But he understands that life in New Orleans is not always gentle. We have discussed the matter and he has agreed to let me arrange for some self-defense training for you."

"Like boxing lessons?" I loved Pappy and would do whatever he asked, but I was not crazy about that idea.

"Not boxing, Dué. That is a sport with rules. Self-defense is not a sport, and there is but one rule—survival. I have a friend who will teach this to you."

I did not understand and said so.

"It'll be good for you." He nodded, and I understood that the decision had already been made. "I have an idea. A long time ago, when I used to fish in the lake, I would fish under the bridge lights. Bugs are drawn to light. They'd hit the light, get zapped and fall into the water. I caught a lot of fish under those lights."

"No lights out here, Pappy."

He raised a finger. "There could be." He pointed to a small tree about 25 yards away.

"I brought a Coleman gas-powered lantern along to have extra light in the evening, but I think it could serve a better purpose." He scratched the side of his face. "What if, right at dusk, we hung the lantern in that tree and let it burn all night, or at least until it ran out of fuel? Who knows, come morning there might be a fish or two hanging out there, snacking on dead bugs, waiting to be caught for breakfast."

We started our campfire and prepared the clubhouse for the evening. Pappy had already sprayed the interior for mosquitoes and retrieved the mosquito nets and candles from the hiding place. We had covered all of the openings with nets. Now, with dusk approaching, we lit the citronella candles to keep the bugs at bay.

We paddled across the swamp to the tree Pappy had selected. I steadied the pirogue and Pappy secured the lantern to a branch that hung over the water. It took several attempts for Pappy to get the Coleman lantern burning. I learned a couple of new words during that process.

By the time we returned to the campsite, we were well past hungry. For dinner we cooked hot dogs over the fire and warmed a can of pork and beans at the edge of the fire pit.

"Situation like this, you want your troops close by. I'll sleep in the clubhouse with you."

He didn't ask if I was scared. Pappy made it seem like we were soldiers together. No question that he was in charge, but he acted as if we were two men on a mission, not a scared kid and his grandfather.

When I stretched out in my sleeping bag, a strange thing happened. Here I was, out in the swamp with my grandfather, hiding from a criminal, and guess who popped into my thoughts?

Yeah, it was Cheryl, but not in the way you'd think. If I let Pappy's word for the criminal slip in front of Cheryl, she'd get really upset. I would have to be very careful with my language so as not to make a mistake. The other option would be to explain the situation to her the way Pappy had explained it to me. Tell her I'd do my best, but might make a slip. That was the big internal debate that put me to sleep.

Chapter 16

The sky exploded around midnight. I sat up in my sleeping bag. Pappy leaned against the opening to the clubhouse watching the show. It was a multi-media event: cypress trees swayed in violent gusts of wind and rain. Occasional hail pellets slammed against the walls of the clubhouse. The entire scene was illuminated by constant flashes of lightning. I joined him at the doorway.

"Something to see, right, boy?"

"Yes, sir."

Pappy placed his hand on my shoulder. "I was almost asleep when the first gust hit the clubhouse. About the same time, I smelled and tasted the sweetness of coming rain. I got up to enjoy the storm."

"Pretty wild."

The wind howled through the trees.

"I'll bet the gusts are near 60 miles an hour, Dué. A storm like this in the city might not even awaken us, but out here it is spectacular. You should see one at sea."

All of a sudden, memories of stories Mom had told me at bedtime came to mind. Instead of kid stories, she had spun tales about a sea captain. Were they stories she made up, or were they about her father, my Pappy?

I loved Pappy and knew he'd do anything for me, but I was hesitant to ask him about what Dad had described as Pappy's other life. I can't explain why. Being a kid with an active imagination, maybe I had read between the lines as Dad had touched upon those days. Or, maybe I was afraid Pappy had done some bad things, and I didn't want to know about them. Whatever the reason, I did not feel comfortable asking him, but surely did want to remember the stories Mom had told.

When the storm subsided, I said goodnight and returned to my sleeping bag. I tried to relax and see if the stories would play in my imagination.

The wind continued to howl. I was trying to recall Mom's stories. I was drifting between asleep and awake when I heard another sound. It took a second for the new sound to process in my brain. It was Pappy humming, though not loudly enough to awaken me if I had been truly asleep. It was a melody I had heard somewhere before. "What are you singing, Pappy?"

"Didn't realize you were awake. Just an old song."

I leaned up on an elbow. "It sounds familiar. More like a hymn."

The sound of his chuckle drifted across the room. "A hymn is nothing more than a song we sing in church."

Church and Pappy were two words that did not go together. The only times I had ever seen him in church were special events such as when I received the math award and when I served my first Mass as an altar boy. And, of course, he was there for Mom's funeral.

After a little while, I remembered the words to the hymn: *I see the stars, I hear the rolling thunder, the power of the universe displayed. Then sings my soul, my Savior God to Thee.*

How Great Thou art—I finished that one verse. "That sure applies here, doesn't it, Pappy?"

"That's probably why I was humming the tune, boy."

Dad had said that a person's religion was not something open for discussion. I thought about what a fine man my grandfather was, wondered why he did not go to church.

My mind worked that puzzle until sleep grabbed me.

Chapter 17

We were up before dawn. As the first ray of sunlight cracked the eastern sky, we slipped the pirogue into the water and paddled toward the lantern. As Pappy had predicted, it ran out of fuel during the night.

"Let's see if our idea was any good," Pappy said. He cast his line, it hit the water, he reached for his pipe, and Bang! The cork disappeared below the surface.

"Damn, Dué, if it ain't a gator, it is one big-ass fish." He grunted with exertion as he worked the fish. When I netted it, we saw it was a humongous green trout. In other parts of the country, people call that fish a bass.

It was large enough to feed both of us. We returned to the campsite for breakfast. Quitting after one fish didn't make us conservationists or anything. Heck, I don't think that word had been spoken in Louisiana back then, and now it's only whispered. The fact was, we had limited space in the ice chest. There was no point in keeping something we couldn't eat in one meal.

Pappy had brought a couple of rabbit traps. After breakfast, he was showing me how they worked when we heard the cans. We looked at each other, turned and moved toward the pirogue. As we slipped it into the water, we heard a shout above the rattle of the cans.

"Shit, Dué, what the frick is this shit?"

My face split into a grin. "Pappy, that would be Jimmy."

He spit into the water. "Go get your friend, and bring him to the hut. I'll be up in the tree. Do not look up at me."

"What?"

"He may have been followed. Do it, boy, run!"

I ran along the tracks toward Jimmy, hushed him when I got there. We reset the cans he had triggered and walked to the campsite.

Pappy was on the platform in the tree.

"Can you hear me, Dué?" he whispered.

I said we could.

He explained that sound carried in the marsh, and it would be safer to keep our voices down when we spoke with him. "The asshole may not know I am with you. That gives us an edge." After a pause, he asked Jimmy how he knew we were here.

Realizing he had screwed up, Jimmy appeared to be close to tears. "I went to your house to check on you. One of your aunts, I get them mixed up, said you all had gone camping. This seemed like the logical spot. My mom said I could come out here and spend the night with you guys."

When Pappy climbed down the steps we had nailed to the tree, I noticed that they were on the side of the tree not visible from the tracks—accident, or careful planning by my grandfather? With the passing of each hour I was learning that everything Pappy did in the swamp was done for a reason.

I knew Pappy was pissed, but he didn't show it. Jimmy was already sorry enough.

"Not your fault, Jimmy. We should have let everyone know this was a secret." He laughed. "Hell, if you let everyone know, it ain't a secret."

I think that made Jimmy feel better, but he made the offer anyway. "I can leave if you want."

Pappy shook his head. "Absolutely not! If he followed you, and we're not sure of that, you could get in trouble if you met him on the way out. You're in this with us, Jimmy. We'll be fine." He grabbed a canteen of water and a can of peanuts. As he moved, Pappy made sure the clubhouse blocked any view of him from the tracks.

I thought of something: the pirogue would only carry two people. "Pappy, what about the plan?"

He squatted between Jimmy and me. "You always want to be flexible, boys, particularly in combat. If that asshole followed you, combat's just what he'll get. Tell you what. Unless I can think of anything better, if I give the word, Dué, you and Jimmy get in the pirogue and paddle straight for the post office to make that call we discussed."

"What about you, Pappy? What will you do?"

He had crouch-walked to the base of the tree. He looked over his shoulder to answer. "I'm going to make this the absolute worst day in that asshole's life."

Jimmy and I passed the morning in a futile attempt to work on the rabbit traps. We were nervous, and, since we were kids, easily distracted. I whispered to Pappy from the base of the tree and pointed to our fishing poles.

He nodded. Jimmy and I got into the pirogue and paddled to the place where Pappy and I had caught the green trout. Fishing was slow.

"Dué," Jimmy whispered.

"What?"

"Did I tell you what my big brother found out?"

I shook my head. With everything happening, we had not talked in a couple of days.

"There's a deaf priest over at St. Raphael's."

That was the adjoining parish where my grandparents had gone to church before Mom died.

"So what's the big deal about that?"

"My brother goes there to scope out the girls in line for Confession."

I was slow. This made no sense. Why would his brother care who went to Confession? I voiced my opinion.

He grinned. "Because, dummy, a girl who has to stand in a long line so she can confess her sins to a deaf priest is the kind of girl we want to know."

My smile rivaled the previous evening's lightning show. My sin could be forgiven. You see, it was not that God would not forgive my sin. The problem was that the sin was so bad—dirty thoughts about a nun—that I could not confess it. No Confession, no forgiveness. It's a Catholic thing. But if the priest was truly deaf and they were letting him hear Confessions, I could be saved.

If Pappy had not been there, even with the threat of the asshole wanting to kill me, I would have left the swamp, run home, and pedaled my bike to St. Raphael's. I had never been on God's bad side before, and I wanted to get back where I belonged as soon as possible.

My thoughts were interrupted by a splash. Not a fish. Pappy had thrown a cypress ball near us.

I looked up.

He made a quiet sign with his lips, pointed at me, and indicated I should join him on the platform in the tree.

Pappy handed his binoculars to me. "Dué, a car pulled up and stopped right where the road crosses the tracks. I can only see the front half, but it's a Hudson Hornet. The driver hasn't gotten out. He's parked next to Jimmy's bike."

I tried to focus the glasses, but my hands were shaking.

If Pappy noticed, he didn't say so.

"Take your time, watch the car. When he gets out, see if you can recognize him. We have to be sure."

I nodded and watched.

He spoke to me in a quiet, reassuring voice.

"We have two plans to consider, son. If he starts down the tracks now, before dark, I want you two to get in that pirogue and paddle as fast as you can to the post office. If I were a betting man, I'd wager that he is going to wait for dark, sneak up on us."

I saw his smile. "And that's a good thing?"

"Real good, Dué. If he doesn't make his move by dusk, I want you and Jimmy to make a lot of noise about going fishing. As soon as you can no longer see the camp, he won't be able to see you. Paddle like hell for that telephone."

"You'll be all right, Pappy?"

He touched my arm. "I will. He won't."

"Pappy, he's getting out of the car."

"Keep watching, let me know what he's doing, everything you see."

I provided a narrative. "Still can't see his face. He has a big bottle of water."

"Do you see a gun?"

"Think there is a pistol in one hand." I paused. "Yep, he put the pistol and the water bottle on the roof of his car."

"The roof?"

"That's right. He stepped on the hood and climbed to the roof."

I watched as he sat on the roof and turned to face us. I would never forget that face. I felt a surge of something within me. It was fear for sure, but there was excitement too.

"Pappy, I think he's on the roof so he can see over the marsh grass."

"Does it look like he has binocs?"

"No, sir. He has his hand over his eyes, like protecting them from the sun."

Pappy nudged me. "Go on down with Jimmy, move around, make sure he sees you two. I want you to look like two kids playing at a campsite."

I looked at Pappy. "Like we're bait?"

He smiled. "Sort of, son, but don't you fret. He's only got a pistol and can't hurt you from there. You and Jimmy will be long gone before he makes his move."

It took forever for the afternoon to pass.

Pappy came down from the tree shortly before dusk. We did the "fishing thing" as he had instructed: talked in loud voices about fishing, made a big production of hauling gear to the pirogue.

Pappy sat near the edge of the water, placed his hand in the mud, and rubbed it on his arms. In a few minutes, anyplace not covered by clothing was covered with mud. This was my first lesson in camouflage.

"You boys best be going. Remember, as long as you can look back and see me or the camp, you are fishermen. As soon as you can't, haul ass for that phone booth."

I didn't know what to say.

Pappy did. "Maybe in the morning we can catch another big trout for breakfast."

Chapter 18

We did our best to pretend that we were looking for a place to fish on our way to the post office. We wanted to paddle super-fast but didn't want to tip over. While the night was dark, the water was way past that.

Luck was with us. Every few minutes, the lights of cars on the old road served as beacons to keep us on course for the highway. The swamp around us was a shade darker than pitch. I was glad we had not brought a flashlight because all we would have seen were pin-points of red watching us—gators.

Having spent a lot of time in the outdoors, we knew that alligators did not want to be around humans. Unless you had the misfortune of trespassing into an area they had staked out for their young, their normal action was to retreat.

We beached the pirogue and ran along the levee to the post office. About half-way there, we heard a shot.

I stopped.

Jimmy shoved me. "Run, Dué, run. If that's what we think it was, Pappy needs help quick."

We resumed the sprint to the telephone. I lifted the receiver, prayed for a dial tone, got one and dialed "O."

The phone rang twice. "Operator, may I help you?"

"Third District Police, please. It's an emergency," I panted into the mouthpiece. I was out of breath from the run. Guess I sounded scared. She transferred the call without questions.

"Third District."

"This is Dué Bonogura. Do you know my dad?"

"Yes, I do. He's in the command center upstairs. I'll get him."

There was a clicking noise in my ear as the call transferred. "Dad, the bad guy is here on the island. Pappy sent us to call for help. He's going to follow him."

"Where are you?"

"Jimmy and I are at the post office on the old highway. Pappy said to come here to call. Dad, I am pretty sure we heard a gunshot."

"We're on the way, son. I want you and Jimmy to stay out of sight behind the post office until we get there."

It seemed like a long time, but was probably not more than 10 minutes before we heard the approach of sirens.

Jimmy and I jumped into the back seat of the first car.

"Which way, boys?" the driver asked.

We gave directions to the road-railroad intersection. The asshole's car had not moved. I pointed to it.

"You two stay in this car until we come for you. Your dad will be along in a second."

A second car skidded to a stop. Four police in full riot gear charged out. Dad was in the third car.

The police had left the lights flashing but had turned the sirens off. That was a good thing. Otherwise, they would not have heard Pappy.

"Relax. It's over." His voice came from somewhere along the tracks.

You know the police. Once they start the charge, it's hard to stop them.

The first two tripped one of Pappy's can alarms. They became tangled in the fishing line and fell in a jumble of twine, police gear, and tin cans.

Above the cursing of the officers, I promise I heard Pappy say, "Shit."

Dad said he thought it best for us to stay in the car for a few minutes. He jogged along the track and acted as a go-between for Pappy and the police.

Dad returned. I could see his smile in the headlights of the police car. "Now that they realize we're all on the same team, I think everyone's safe."

Even though I had heard Pappy's voice, I had to ask the question. "Is Pappy okay?"

"Pappy's fine, son."

"Did they get the bad guy?" See, I did not say that "a" word in front of my dad.

Dad nodded. "Yes."

One of the officers returned to the car and pulled a piece of black plastic from the trunk. "Give me a couple of minutes before you go to see your grandpa."

"Is he okay?" Even though Dad had said it, the body bag scared me. I wanted reassurance.

"He's great. This is for the other guy."

Dad rummaged around in the car and found a working flashlight.

We followed him along the track. A few paces beyond the second trap Pappy and I had set, we came upon the plastic sheet covering what I guessed was a body.

Pappy sat at the campfire, speaking with the police officers. The two who had become entangled in the trap were being razzed by the others.

Pappy waved at me. "Come here, boy."

I walked toward him.

He embraced me in a bear hug. "You did real good, Dué. The police got here quick." He pushed me to arms' length, looked me in the eye. "We don't need to worry about that"—he winked—"*asshole* anymore."

Pappy had a blue metal coffee pot on the edge of the fire. The officers helped themselves to the strong brew. Jimmy and I sat on the porch in front of the clubhouse and listened to the adults. I'm not sure if Jimmy and I realized this at the time, but if kids are quiet around grown-ups, sometimes the grown-ups forget about the kids and say some pretty interesting things.

When, for example, the detective in charge of the investigation sent two of the uniformed police to the other side of the swamp to retrieve the pirogue, one of the other officers said, "grab a couple of six packs."

While things are different in New Orleans today, they were really different back then.

Jimmy and I held our silence and enjoyed the stories which came off the beer-loosened tongues.

From what we heard, Pappy had stayed out of sight on the west side of the island and had waited near the second trap. The piles of shells and the fact that he had covered himself with mud made him pretty much invisible. And, just like the police, the killer had tripped and become tangled in the line.

That was when Pappy hit the asshole's arm with the bat. The force of the blow knocked the gun free and accounted for the shot we'd heard. There must have been a fight, because the other guy was dead. One of the police said Pappy had broken the asshole's neck.

I looked at my grandfather. Pappy did have huge forearms, strong hands.

An officer who had enjoyed more than his share of beer had said, "Son of a bitch broke the Lieutenant's Rule Number One."

We listened.

"Yep, before you go to an ass-kicking contest, first be real sure who's gonna supply the ass."

At that point, Dad said it was late and asked if one of the officers could give us a ride home.

During the drive, I asked my dad if Pappy would be in any trouble.

"Dué, there is something in the law called 'self-defense.' If you feel your life is in danger, you are allowed to use whatever means necessary to defend yourself."

The policeman driving the car reinforced Dad's statement. "Trouble? I'd like to see if we could give him a medal."

Jimmy said, "Cool."

Chapter 19

I don't think the word "sleep" is adequate to describe what I did that night. Coma might be a better description of the state I was in.

The phone rang at eight o'clock. I opened one eye, thought about letting it ring. Whoever was calling would eventually give up. Wrong.

It was probably Dad calling from work. He had another accounting job on Saturday mornings at a neighborhood drug store. I climbed out of bed and walked the seven steps from my bed to the phone.

"Hello," I mumbled into the phone.

"Anthony?"

It was Cheryl.

I yawned. "Hi."

"Did I wake you?"

Girls can ask dumb questions. "Yeah, but that's okay."

"Mom made me wait until eight to make the call, but we've been listening to the news. I was worried."

I rubbed my eyes to chase away sleep. "We're all fine. Well, not the bad guy, but Pappy, Jimmy, and I are all good."

"Can you come over?"

"Now?"

"No, silly. Can you have lunch with us?"

"I'll have to ask Dad."

"Granny's making rabbit stew."

I laughed. "Change that. I'll beg my dad."

"Anthony, listen."

I did and heard a scratching sound on the phone. It was her knuckles rubbing across the mouthpiece. I said, "Me too," and rubbed mine.

In a very soft voice, she said, "See you."

The bed looked mighty good, but if I climbed back in, I would return to that deep, empty sleep. I might or might not wake up in time for lunch, which would mean missing the rabbit stew.

My first stop was the bathroom. I brushed my teeth and thought of Joey's face-washing procedure as I scrubbed mine. I smiled, dressed, and called Dad.

"Morning, Dad."

He sounded as tired as I felt. "Hi, son, I'm surprised you're up this early."

"I got a phone call. Cheryl wanted to know if I could join them for lunch. Told her I'd have to ask you."

He was six blocks away on the other end of the phone line, but I could see his smile—the good one. "Anything I should know about that, Dué?"

"Sure wish I knew what to say, Dad. I mean, the guys would kill me if they heard this, but I like being with her."

"I hear another 'but' in there, son."

I laughed. "You're right, Dad. I feel real good when I'm with her, but I also feel stupid. I always say the wrong thing, come up with the wrong answers to her questions. So, why do I like to be with her?"

The smile I knew but couldn't see turned to a laugh. "It's starting, son. It's most definitely starting. If Aunt Rose hasn't fixed anything for your lunch, you can go."

"Thanks."

I walked to the back yard and opened the shed, where the policeman had dumped my bike after the asshole tried to run over me.

The rear fender was beyond hope. The tire rim was bent, but with my spoke-adjusting tool and a hammer I was able to make it functional. The job took longer than I had expected, and the bike retained a bit of a wobble. I would fine-tune it later. For now, the sweat rolling off my face dictated the need for a bath.

Other than for her cousin's party, I'd never taken any great pains to look nice, get cleaned up, or comb my hair before visiting Cheryl.

This time, though, I was almost "church clean" when I leaned my bike against the side of her house.

She was on the big swing in her back yard. When she saw me, she jumped off and ran toward me. Even after all these years, that picture remains perfectly clear. Her hair, fastened with a yellow ribbon, was pulled back in her usual ponytail. The ribbon matched her shirt.

She wore bright white shorts. Can white be bright? Her shorts were really white. It may have looked that way because of the contrast with the tan of her legs. For a skinny, straight-line girl, she had some nice legs—from all the basketball, I guessed.

She ran up to me, wrapped her arms around me, and gave a great hug and a better kiss.

I didn't know what to do with my hands. Her parents were home and all, but it seemed natural to place my arms around her. To my delight, she didn't pull away. It seemed that she held me tighter.

"Anthony, I was so scared."

God forbid I miss the opportunity to screw something up! My right hand sort of slipped. No, I didn't break any rules, did nothing I would have to confess—besides, it was accidental. My right hand fell down her back to her waist, right above where her butt started the curve thing.

Her eyes locked on mine. "Anthony, if your hand moves any lower, I will break it."

I pulled the offending hand away as if it had hit hot coals in the barbecue. I said it was an accident, but even to me, my explanation sounded like babbling.

She smiled, touched my cheek, and suggested we go inside for lunch. Just before we reached the door, she stopped and issued an unexpected briefing.

"Mom knows about us, likes you, and is okay with everything. We don't know how Dad would feel, so he doesn't know." A wink. "Dad doesn't have a clue."

The correct response would have been that I should sit by her dad—he and I had something in common.

Her message conveyed, Cheryl turned and walked up the five steps to her kitchen. Along came a distraction. The back of her shorts—not too short-short, but just right—became the center of my attention.

Pappy had been 100% correct when he had said she would fill

out nice.

More questions came to mind. Why did God create something so cute on one day, and on the next day, rule that it was a sin to touch or even think about it? If girls didn't want you to pay any attention to it, why did they wear tight shorts?

But the big question was this. Was Cheryl going from straight lines to curves overnight or was it that I was starting to notice things? My life had become a series of questions without answers.

Granny's rabbit stew didn't provide any answers, but the flavor of that brown gravy pushed all other thoughts aside. To this date, it's the absolute best thing I've ever tasted—barely edging out my first experience with oysters, baked Sicilian style.

"Dué?"

I swallowed, wiped my mouth with the napkin and looked across the table to Cheryl's dad. "Sir?"

He nodded in Granny's direction. "I can see you're enjoying the stew, but when you finish, could you tell us more of what happened last night? The news coverage on WWL radio was rather spotty."

I sipped at my iced tea—sweet tea, for the record. "Don't really know where to start."

Mrs. Wolf said, "Take your time, Dué."

Granny said, "Let the boy finish his stew. I like to watch him eat."

"Mrs. Wolf, this is better than ice cream."

"You can call me Granny, like everyone else does." She spooned more stew into my plate. I used the time required to devour my third helping to plan what to say and how to say it.

"After the bad guy"—I did not use Pappy's word—"tried to run me over with his car, Dad thought it best to place me in hiding until the police could catch him. Pappy and Dad talked it over and decided that our clubhouse in the swamp was the safest place.

"Pappy was careful on our way there to be sure we weren't followed, but one of my aunts told Jimmy where we were. The bad guy must have followed Jimmy.

"As soon as Jimmy arrived, Pappy figured we would have a problem and developed a plan. He didn't think the guy would come until after dark. Right at twilight, he asked Jimmy and me to act like we were going fishing in the pirogue. When we were out of sight, we paddled to the far edge of the swamp and ran to a telephone booth at the post office."

Granny interrupted. "Must have been pitch black in that swamp."

"It was, Granny. If it hadn't been for the lights of passing cars on the road, we might have gotten lost."

"Were you frightened, Anthony?" Mrs. Wolf asked. "You had seemed so brave after he tried to run you down in the car."

"I think when you saw me, I was too excited to be scared. That boat ride was a different thing. I was worried about Pappy. We knew the bad guy had a pistol. Pappy had a baseball bat and a knife."

"That's all?" Mr. Wolf raised his eyebrows.

"My dad said there was more to Pappy than most people knew. Looks like Dad was right.

"By the time the police arrived, it was over. Pappy was okay and the bad guy was dead."

Cheryl was seated to my left. I felt her hand reach under the table for mine and squeeze it.

"Dead?" Mr. Wolf asked. "How?"

"From what I heard the police say, Pappy used the bat to knock the gun away and then the two of them fought. Pappy won."

Mr. Wolf nodded. "Finding Father Pete and now this! That's more than enough excitement for a lifetime, Dué. Remind me not to get in a fight with your grandfather."

He paused as if carefully selecting his words. "Dué, it's never a good thing to rejoice over the death of another person. We're all glad that you're safe, but a man died."

I wanted to say it was either the asshole or Pappy, but this was Cheryl's dad. I said nothing. My dad had said it was never a good idea for kids to argue with grown-ups.

"And now that he's dead, we'll never know why he killed Father Pete."

I guessed it was okay to answer. "Mr. Wolf, the police had an idea about that. One of the lieutenants recognized the bad guy as some Mafioso he had arrested in the past. Dad's pal, a sergeant, said that maybe a criminal went to Father Pete for Confession, and the other guys in his gang were afraid he told Father some secret things."

"Will they ever know?" Granny asked.

I nodded. "Maybe. The sergeant said that if in the next few days some Mafia guy turns up dead, we'll know who went to Confession."

It was quiet until Mrs. Wolf said, "I think this would be a good time for us to say a prayer of thanksgiving for Dué and his grandfather."

We did.

Mr. Wolf asked Cheryl to clean the table while he and his wife ran some errands. Granny walked toward the living room with a crossword puzzle. I helped Cheryl with the dishes. When we were done, we walked out to the swing in the backyard.

"That was an awesome meal," I said.

She laughed. "I stopped counting after you thanked Granny for the fifth time."

We pushed the swing back and forth.

I turned to her. "Cheryl, there's something I have to tell you."

Bingo! Just that quick, I saw tears form in her eyes. "What?" I asked. "What did I do?"

"You're about to break up with me."

Me and the pogo stick were back in the minefield—no idea how I got here and certainly no idea of a pathway out. "Why would you say that?"

"Because that's how it is in all the books. When the man tells the woman he has to tell her something and acts all serious, he tells her it's over."

I offered a prayer of thanks before I answered. There were books about this! I could read them and learn what to do. I grabbed her wrist, folded her hand into a fist and did our knuckle thing.

"That isn't what's happening. You're not even close. I had promised to do something with Jimmy this afternoon and wanted to tell you about it."

The tears disappeared as suddenly as they had arrived. How did she do that?

"What are you and Jimmy going to do?"

This was my first foray into deception with a female—not a lie, but not the whole story. If I had said I was going to find a deaf priest to hear my Confession because my sin was too great to confess, she would have broken up with me. "Jimmy and I are going to take a long bike ride."

She shrugged. "That's not very important. Why make a big production of telling me?"

I tried a grin. "There is a good chance that I'll find Jimmy someplace you do not want me to be."

She was quick, and not just on the basketball court. "Ashley's." Not a question, a statement.

I nodded, worked the grin again. "Remember when you came to see me after Joey beat me up? I seem to recall you threatening me with even more injury if you found me hanging around with Ashley."

She did the look-through-the-eyelash thing that always got me. "I was upset."

"Well, I didn't want you to hear that I was at Ashley's and get the wrong idea." I paused. "Tell you what. Follow me."

I took her hand to help her off the swing and walked to the side of the garage, a place where we couldn't be seen from either the house or the street. "Hey, you're my pal, my friend. I want to do whatever I can to keep it that way."

I really thought I had said the right words.

She shook her head slowly from side to side. "I hope I'm more than that." She planted the most awesome kiss ever on my lips.

I could taste that kiss all the way to Jimmy's.

Chapter 20

I had guessed correctly. Jimmy, along with several other guys, was at Ashley's. There were a couple of girls there, too. Everybody was sitting on her back porch. Tony was in the place of honor next to Ashley. Mick was several places down the line.

I waved. "Hi."

Ashley stood, and immediately I understood the reason for the crowd. At school, in her uniform, some curves were visible, others were implied. She was wearing cut-off jeans and a very tight t-shirt.

She walked up to me. "Well here's our hero."

I shook my head. "Nope, Pappy was the hero. Jimmy and I were in charge of our escape."

She was close enough for me to smell her perfume. I tried to keep my eyes on her face, but it was a chore. I believe she sensed my discomfort. In a voice loud enough for the crowd to hear, she announced, "That's not what I heard. Jimmy said you were a rock!"

And in a lower voice, just for me: "Is that lipstick on your lips from Cheryl?"

I doubled over as if laughing at a secret joke. The move served two purposes: it hid my blush and gave me the chance to wipe my hand across my lips to remove whatever was there. I looked at my hand—nothing. She had tricked me. Cheryl had not worn lipstick.

Now Ashley was laughing, and everyone wanted to know the joke. She gave me a peck on the cheek, and yes, she did wear lipstick. "A private joke," she said, "between me and Dué."

Before she moved to return to her rightful place in the center of the group, she touched my cheek where she had kissed me. "You better remove that before you visit any basketball players we know."

Wow! If Cheryl hadn't held a hammerlock on my heart, I would have been right in line with the rest of the guys. Ashley was not just a knockout; she was fun. My first thought was that I couldn't wait to share the story with Cheryl. Fortunately, I had a second thought.

I nodded in Jimmy's direction and pointed at my watch. It took a second for him to remember our plans. He told the group that he and I had something we needed to do. They assumed this business was related to the previous night's events, and we knew better than to correct them.

Conversation on the bike ride consisted mainly of Jimmy's opinion of various parts of Ashley's anatomy. "I tell you, Dué, one day she'll be even more awesome than Colleen."

In our circle of friends and related experiences, there was no higher compliment.

We arrived at St. Raphael's, placed our bikes in the rack, and locked them.

When we entered the church, Jimmy said, "That's weird."

"What?" I whispered.

He pointed in the right corner. "That's where Father Rogo hears Confessions. There are only three people in line."

"So?"

"There are four in line for the other priest. Usually everybody's in Father Rogo's line."

"Well, it's early." I tried to sound casual. "Tell you what. Before the line gets too long, I think I'll go."

I walked across the church and took my place in line. By the time you get to church, you pretty much know what sins you have to confess. We Catholics use the time in line for a last minute Examination of Conscience—a time to review, make sure you haven't forgotten any sins, and line-up what you want to say so as to be ready for the priest.

I had only one sin to confess so I passed the time in line thinking of how Jimmy's brother had said things worked with the deaf priest. Fr. Rogo must have been able to hear some sounds because Jimmy's brother had said that when you stopped talking, the priest would go on to the next part of the ritual.

It was my turn. I pushed the curtain aside and took my place on the kneeler. Faint murmurs came through the sound-proofing. The small door behind the screen opened with a creak.

"Place yourself in God's presence in the name of the Father, the Son, and the Holy Spirit."

Out of reflex I nodded and started. "Bless me Father, for I have sinned. It has been a week since my last Confession."

I paused for a breath of courage, and I started my story.

Priests are supposed to be calm individuals, people who have heard every sin we are capable of committing. On top of that, this priest was supposed to be deaf. There was no way I could have known that hours before my visit to Fr. Rogo's confessional, his new hearing aid had arrived.

When I whispered my sin, he exploded.

"You what ?" he screamed.

After a lecture that went on forever, my sweaty, glowing-red face and I found a pew on the far side of the church, where I started my penance, three rosaries.

I found Jimmy waiting outside.

"Holy crap, Dué! I didn't think we were old enough to commit a sin that big. When that priest yelled at you, everybody in church and for a couple of blocks around knew some serious ass sin just got confessed."

He was Catholic enough not to ask the sin, but he did ask what I had gotten for a penance.

Chapter 21

Jimmy returned to Ashley's. I'd be fibbing if I said I had no interest in joining him, but we were a small group. I'd bet that before I could set the kickstand on my bike, somebody would be on the phone to Cheryl.

It wasn't that I was afraid of her. She was my friend. Okay, she was my girlfriend, and I knew it would upset her if I spent the rest of the afternoon with the other guys at Ashley's house.

I wanted to see Cheryl but didn't want her folks to think I was spending too much time over there.

A solution came to mind: I'd ride past her house. If she was outside, we could talk. Maybe I'd get invited in for a visit.

When I was about three houses away, I heard the basketball bouncing on the court. I'd get to watch her, maybe talk a little after she finished.

So as not to disturb her during practice, I parked my bike out of sight of the court. I walked to the big magnolia tree across the street from her house to watch. She was so near-sighted that if I stayed close to the tree, she would probably not notice me.

But I noticed something: she wasn't playing alone. A guy was with her.

I should have left immediately or waited to speak with her, but I was too surprised to think with anything resembling reason. I watched.

He was taller and looked older, at least ninth grade. And he was good. When he was on offense, he could drive to the basket or shoot from outside at will. On defense, he dominated.

I walked back to my bike and pedaled home. I wasn't angry, but I was hurt.

On the other hand, it made sense. She was a great athlete, I was a math geek. Those straight lines of hers that were turning to curves must have caught the attention of some high school jock.

I shook my head. It had been a great couple of weeks, but I

guessed it was over.

There was no point in joining the Ashley parade. There were too many guys in the running; besides, Ashley was a good student, so my math skills would not be any help.

It took Dad all of five minutes to realize I was down. "Hey pal, what's the problem?"

I shrugged.

"Let me guess. Could this have anything to do with a cute little basketball player?"

I nodded.

"Want to talk about it?"

"There's not much to say, Dad."

"Let's start with what happened."

"I think she broke up with me."

Dad gave me a puzzled look. "You think? I'd imagine that would be something pretty straightforward. What did she say?"

"She didn't say anything, Dad."

"Now I'm confused. Dué, if she didn't say anything, how do you know she broke up with you?"

I told him what had happened.

"And you didn't talk to her? You just left?"

I nodded.

"Dué, the other guy could have been a relative. He could have been some new kid in her neighborhood who saw the basketball goal and asked to play."

"I didn't think about that." He had a point. I should have talked to her.

"Son, here's a piece of advice. As you go through this life there will always be people around to give you things to worry about. Don't you be one of them ."

I tried to take Dad's advice to bed with me, but self-pity is a powerful drug. There was always the priesthood.

Yeah, I know: Catholic boy gets jilted, so he decides to become a priest. Like I am the first guy to ever follow that line of thinking! But, it made sense for me. I did a good job as an altar boy and liked working around the church. Now that I had been to Confession to the no-longer-deaf priest, I was back on God's good team.

Father Pete's funeral was scheduled for the next day. It had been delayed so that his brother, also a priest, could return from his work at a mission school in Africa to attend the service. There would probably be a lot of young priests and seminarians at the church. Maybe I could speak with one of them to see what it was really like.

I drifted off to sleep with thoughts of life in the seminary.

Chapter 22

We waited in class for Sister Mary Mercy to arrive to march us to our assigned places in church for the funeral.

She stopped in the doorway. "Dué, come here please."

I walked toward her, careful to avoid eye contact with Cheryl. "Yes, Sister?"

"Would you like to serve at the Mass?"

Sister received my first smile since I had seen Cheryl and her basketball friend.

"Thank you, Sister."

"You should thank Sister Mary John." She touched my eye. "There was a feeling in the convent that we should have an altar server who did not look like he had been hit by a bus." She smiled. "Sister Mary John said that the Holy Spirit had allowed you to find Father Pete and that it must have been Jesus Himself who gave you the courage to act as you did with the police."

Sister Mary Mercy delivered me to Deacon Andrew, the seminarian in charge of the funeral. "Dué, your job will be to carry the crucifix in the procession and to stand with it at the foot of the coffin during the service."

"Yes, Deacon."

"The service will be long, perhaps over an hour. Can you stand still for that long?"

"Yes, sir."

He chuckled. "Do you get in fights very often?"

I shook my head. "No, sir."

"How long ago was the fight?" He motioned for me to walk with him toward the sacristy.

"A few days," I said.

"I am assuming that you lost."

That merited a laugh. "Even worse than that."

The seminarians were using the altar boy change room to don their cassocks. I enjoyed the camaraderie I felt in the group as I put on my cassock and surplice. The priest thing just might work for me.

I picked up the large crucifix, mounted it on the pole we used for processions, and took my place in the line. We processed through the schoolyard to the front of the church, and down the long aisle of church to the altar. As we approached the altar, I stopped at the foot of the casket.

Cheryl was seated at the end of the row next to me. Talk about bad luck!

The service was what we called High Mass, lots of singing and enough incense that at times it looked like a fog bank on the altar. The Abbot from St. Joseph's across the lake gave a brief homily. He said he was deferring to Father Pete's brother, who had prepared a eulogy.

While not a twin, there was no mistaking the family resemblance. Father Pete's brother approached the casket with a gym bag in his hand.

"This is what my brother was all about, finding ways to reach out to our children." He opened the bag, removed a pair of black umpire tennis shoes, and placed them on the coffin.

I was glad everyone was watching him. My eyes filled with tears. They ran down my face as he spoke, but I did my job. I kept both hands on the crucifix. Try as I may, I don't recall much of the eulogy. The tennis shoes did me in.

The schoolyard and church were deserted by the time we returned from the cemetery. I removed and hung my cassock and surplice in the locker, checked the candles on the altar, and stepped out the back door of the sacristy.

I heard the sound of a basketball striking the backboard. Cheryl caught the ball and walked over to me.

"Hi," she said.

I watched her walk toward me. Man, she was pretty. She had the ability to hurt my feelings, but I didn't think I could ever be angry with her. "Hi."

"Anthony, I was so proud of you."

"Thanks."

"I asked Mom if I could stay at school to wait for you. I know how upset you were during the service."

I explained about the tennis shoes.

"You and everyone else. I hope you don't have any plans. I told Mom you would walk me home."

I thought "crap" but said, "sure."

We walked across the schoolyard toward Gentilly Boulevard. That was the most direct route. A small park, more of a vacant lot with a couple of swing sets, marked the halfway point. It was a quiet walk. Silence had never been an uncomfortable thing for us, but this one was strained.

Cheryl touched my arm. "Let's take a break."

She did not wait for an answer, but walked over to one of the swings, brushed some dust off the wood seat, and sat.

Not knowing what else to do, I followed her.

"Something's wrong, Anthony. Something besides the funeral."

I did the usual: I nodded.

"Do you remember the night when you got all serious and I cried?"

"Yes."

"I was afraid you were going to break up with me, but I am not too worried about that anymore. I know you care for me."

"Yeah, right."

"What's that supposed to mean?"

"You know."

She stopped the swing, stood and faced me.

"Anthony, one of the things I love about us is that we talk. My girlfriends complain that their boyfriends never talk. You've always been open with me. What's this about?"

I exhaled. "After Jimmy and I finished our ride, he went back to Ashley's. I didn't want to go there. I wanted to see you."

She held up her hand. "Stop. Let me guess. You passed my house and saw me playing basketball with a guy."

I looked at the ground.

"Anthony, if I didn't spend most of my time planning my outfits to look nice for you, I would beat you with a stick."

I wasn't just back in the minefield on my pogo stick—I felt as if I were blindfolded too.

"I don't know why you're mad at me."

"Well, let me clear that up. When I arrived at school this morning, two of my friends were eager to tell me about a private moment you and Ashley shared. Did I get angry? Was I afraid you were breaking up with me? No! I was confidant of the feelings we have for each other and knew you would have an explanation. And we will discuss that later!"

Oops.

"What do I have to do to convince you how I feel about you? We can't have you getting all jealous or angry every time you see me with someone else. If I get an invitation to a party and we don't have anything planned, I'll probably accept. That doesn't mean you aren't my boyfriend. It means that we're too young to go steady."

"I'm sorry."

"That's fine, but I'm not finished."

Her face was flushed. She was angry. I wanted to hold her in my arms.

"The boy you saw me with was the son of a coach. The coach happens to be the man who's forming the new all-city girl's basketball team. That was my tryout for the team. The coach has his son go one-on-one with the candidates. He watches and grades performance."

I didn't know what to do. Talk about feel stupid! I held out my hand to her. "I'm an idiot, Cheryl. I'm sorry. How did it go?"

She shrugged. "I was one of the first to try out. He said we'd hear from him in a few weeks."

"Wow. An all-city team, that's got to feel great."

She took my hand, closed it into a fist and rubbed hers against it. "It's only great if my boyfriend is happy about it."

"He is," I said.

"Anthony, I have an idea. I think it'll help us avoid anything like this in the future." She pressed her knuckles hard against mine. "If anyone asks me out, I'll tell you right away. And if I were to ever start to like someone else, I would tell you. Until that happens, you have nothing to worry about. How does that sound? Will that help you relax?"

I placed my other hand on top of our knuckle thing. "Yes. That will help."

"And?"

"And what?"

She gave me that eyelash look. "You could promise the same thing."

I thought about that. "Cheryl, I could say the words, but they wouldn't mean anything because I can't imagine meeting anyone I'd rather be with than you."

"Anthony, that was beautiful." She released my hand, placed her hands on my face and kissed me.

She ended the kiss and winked. "And now we'll discuss the time you spent with Ashley."

For once in my life, I was glad I knew nothing about girls. I lacked the experience to expect any success at deceit and told her the whole story, including the peck on the cheek. I did sort of wince at telling her that part, though.

Instead of a smack, I received a great smile as she extended her fist for the knuckle brush.

"I knew I could trust you, Anthony. That is exactly what I was told."

I shook my head. "You talked to Ashley?"

"No, silly, one of the other girls who was there was happy to tell me about Ashley and my boyfriend."

New Orleans is a small town.

Chapter 23

Pappy was waiting on the front porch when I got home from school.

"Put your bike in the shed, boy. We have an appointment."

I did as he said and climbed into the car. "Where we going, Pappy?"

"Today is your first self-defense lesson."

I had mixed feelings about this and guessed Pappy sensed it.

"This ain't a sport, boy. It's about survival. You listen to what Leo has to say, and you may very well have had your ass kicked for the last time."

I grinned. "That part sounds good."

After a short drive, he passed through the rear gate to the Fairgrounds Racetrack. "Didn't know we were going to the zoo," I said.

Pappy laughed.

When I was real little, he'd tell Grandma he was taking me to the zoo. Grandma did not like him going to the track. After a few instances of my telling her about all of the pretty horses I saw at the zoo, she figured it out and he was busted again.

Many of the people who worked at the track lived in trailers—an inexpensive way to follow the racing circuit around the country. The back corner of the trailer park was reserved for the year-round residents.

We parked next to a shiny Airstream. Pappy got out of his car and knocked on the door. He motioned for me to stay in the car and conducted a whispered conversation with someone inside the motor home.

He motioned to me. "Come here, boy. I want you to meet a friend of mine."

I joined him at the trailer door.

"Leo, this is my grandson." He shoved me through the door. "Dué, this is Leo. See you all in an hour or so."

A very slender man extended his hand. "Leo."

I shook his hand. His skin would have made saddle leather seem delicate. "Hi, Mr. Leo. I'm Dué."

"No Mister. Just Leo."

"Yes, sir."

"Follow me." He walked toward a barn.

From his weathered face, I would have guessed that he was much older than Pappy, but he had a bounce to his walk, moved like a much younger man.

"Men fight in here." He slammed his hand on the side of the barn. "They don't box or wrestle. They fight for money—kick, punch, bite, pull, whatever it takes until one of them gets knocked out or quits. That is what I do, boy. I teach men to fight."

I had no idea what to say. "Holy crap," I thought, "what has Pappy gotten me into?"

He looked at me, placed his hand on my shoulder and squeezed it, kind of like my aunts did with fruit and vegetables in the grocery. He asked me to hold up a hand. I did. He studied it as if it were a map. "Yep, your grandfather was right, you ain't gonna be big. Best make a choice, young man. Learn to fight, learn to run away real fast, or count on getting your ass kicked regular."

He answered my question before I could form the words.

"Surprise is the key. Strike first, and make it count. Most fights are won by the man who lands the first blow."

I had never met anyone like Leo.

"Here's an example of what I mean. The thing that happened in the swamp—the killer had a pistol. Your grandfather had a baseball bat and surprise on his side. See who won?"

I nodded. That made sense.

"Let me see you run."

"Sir?" I did not understand.

He pointed at his trailer. "Run to the trailer and back, as fast as you can."

I did.

"Good, you're not too winded. That's the first thing we'll tackle, your legs. Your legs are the most powerful muscles in your body."

For the rest of the hour, Leo described his plan. We would work on something called "wind sprints." These were short runs of 10 to 20 yards, but we would do it on the soft mud of the track to build the muscles on the top of my legs. After that, he would work with me on tactics to create surprise and places on the body he called "pressure points" to attack. The lesson would end with a 30 minute run.

"We're going to work three days a week. On the days we don't work, I want you to run for at least an hour. Our legs are our biggest muscles. We're going to make yours strong enough to hurt someone when you kick them.

"You may not win every fight. That's not my goal. I promise you that when we're done, if anyone gets in a fight with you, they'll know they've been in battle. Chances are, they won't mess with you again."

For the first few lessons, I was convinced that the old man was nuts, but I learned to run and, in time, I learned I was good at it. After the second week of training, I told Pappy I no longer needed a ride. It was a little over three miles from my neighborhood to the track. I ran both ways.

Chapter 24

I had gotten into the habit of stopping at Cheryl's for a glass of water on the way home from the track. And, yes, there was often a cookie involved, and now and then a kiss. She had teased me about being all sweaty when I visited my girlfriend but had threatened to punch me if I by-passed her house. We were on the back yard swing when she dropped the bomb.

"Please don't get upset."

This, of course, meant she was going to say something I would not like.

"What?"

"I have a date tomorrow night."

This was a test and I was determined to pass it. "Thanks for telling me."

Old Mister Silence wedged in between us.

She spoke first. "Anything else?"

I shook my head. "Not unless you tell me I should be worried."

Her smile indicated a passing grade.

"See? That's wonderful. You trust me."

I laughed. "My first thought was to fall to the ground and hold my breath until you agreed to call it off."

She offered her fist. We touched.

"One of my dad's friends has houseguests this weekend. They brought their son with them and would like him to have a date for a party at their house."

"He lives out of town?" I was feeling better.

She nodded.

"So unless you elope, I'm cool?"

Instead of her tiny fist rubbing mine, it punched my shoulder.

No jealousy in this guy, no way. I was one confident young man. The ruse lasted until I was about three blocks from her house. The guy could be rich, cool, a jock. There was such a thing as a long-distance romance. I was screwed.

It would be very romantic to say I tossed and turned all night and didn't sleep, but after running three miles each way to Leo's, plus his workout, the toss and turn thing lasted about a minute.

It was tough to project my calm, self-assured act at school, but I thought I carried it off. That's not quite true. Cheryl caught me at the bike rack after school.

"Dué"—she only used Anthony when we were alone—"no matter how nice you act, I know you're worried. I have an eleven o'clock curfew, but I won't call you tonight. I promise to call you first thing in the morning."

Man, could she ever read me!

While I wasn't sure what the word "paranoia" meant, I knew it would be the featured item on my mental menu for the evening with, of course, a side dish of jealousy.

Just after I got home and was rummaging through the kitchen for a snack, the phone rang. How good was my luck? It might be Cheryl calling to let me know her date had been run over by a bus and couldn't make it.

"Hello," I said with fingers crossed.

"Dué, it's Dad."

Friday was Dad's bowling night. He was probably calling to make sure I was okay with his being out late. He was and always will be the most considerate person I have ever known.

"We have some last-minute reports due and I will most probably work right up to the time I have to leave for the bowling alley. I was thinking, some of the people on my bowling team want to meet you. Why don't you meet me at the alley? I spoke with Aunt Rose, and she is having leftovers tonight. How about pizza at the alley with me?"

A man in my severe state of depression should not have been able to muster a cheer, but pizza instead of the road kill Aunt Rose called leftovers merited one.

"Yahoo!"

Dad laughed. "I take that as a yes. Why don't you meet me at the alley at seven-thirty or so?"

Thinking about being at the bowling alley with my dad distracted me, but the worry forced its way back to the front of my brain. I had some time to kill—not a good thing.

But hold on a second. Cheryl's house was only three blocks from the bowling alley. Her date was picking her up at seven. A plan rolled along the track of my brain like a locomotive coming down the Mississippi River Bridge—no way to stop it.

Here's what I did. Even for me, this was way out there on the stupid farm. I climbed up the magnolia tree across the street from her house and hid there to watch her date's parents pick her up. Maybe her dad would drive her to the party.

My bicep got a workout checking my watch. Of course, there was a chance that I wouldn't get to see anything. The date could have been cancelled.

No, the porch light was on. That meant someone was expected at their house. I had to meet Dad at the bowling alley by seven-thirty. This could be tight, but nothing was getting me out of that tree!

A car came down the street. It was moving very slowly, as if the driver were trying to find house numbers. It stopped in front of Cheryl's house. The driver got out. It was her date!

If Cheryl's date was old enough to drive, I was toast.

The only smart thing I did that night was to get out of the tree and run to the bowling alley. Seeing my girlfriend all dressed up to go to a party with another guy would not have been good.

I found Dad in the locker room changing from his suit into casual clothes.

"Hey, pal. You don't look so great."

"Cheryl has a date tonight."

He shook his head. "I'm sorry, Dué."

"Some friends of her folks brought their son to town."

"So it was a favor to her parents. It's not like she met someone she wanted to date."

"But he's old enough to drive, Dad."

"Well, that's strange. I didn't think her parents would allow her to date anyone that much older. Wait, how did you know that?"

I looked at the floor. "I sort of hung around to see what he looked like."

Dad shook his head. "That was not very bright."

I nodded. "I know."

"Did she see you?"

"No."

"Are you sure? She might be upset if she thought you were spying on her."

"She didn't see me."

He motioned to me. "Come on, pal. Let's go get a pizza."

I stood to follow, but he stopped, looked around the locker room. We were alone.

Dad paused for a second. "Dué, there is something about women I don't really understand."

I laughed. "Hope you are not looking here for answers."

"No, son, I know better. What I have observed is that women, especially the married ones, don't like to see a man remain single. More often than not, the wife of someone on my team or somebody from work will accidentally show up with a friend she wants me to meet. I mention this because I don't want you to be confused this evening. There's a good chance that you'll be introduced to some women. I just want you to know that I'm not dating anybody, and I have no plans to do so."

I was doubled over with laughter.

Dad touched my shoulder. "Are you all right, son?"

"Dad, you're trying to explain women to a guy who spent the better part of an hour in a tree spying on his girlfriend."

Dad sat down. "In a tree?"

"Yep, there's a big magnolia across the street from Cheryl's. That was my hiding place."

I watched his eyes fill with tears. He put his arm around my shoulders and pulled me close to him. "I don't know much about the next life, Dué, but I can promise you that somewhere your mom is busting a gut laughing at us. And I'm sure she'd want to give you a hug like this one."

Dad pulled me real close.

He released me, gave me a wink, and we left the locker room for the snack bar.

We ordered pizza and a Dixie beer for Dad and a root beer for me. The parade started as soon as we placed our order. Within a couple of minutes, three different women came up to our table with friends they knew Dad "just wanted" to meet.

The candidates were easy to pick out—too much hair, way too much make-up, and tighter-fitting clothes than the other ladies. Dad was polite and pleasant but clearly not interested.

They kept coming until the waiter brought our pizza. This wasn't just any pizza. This was pizza with sausage from the guy in Mid-City and olive salad from the grocery in the French Quarter on top of red sauce and cheese!

As part of a male tradition, we burned our mouths with the hot cheese on the pizza. We laughed and made small talk over the background noise of the bowling alley.

When he finished eating, Dad was very careful to clean his hands of the pizza sauce and grease before he picked up his bowling ball and joined his friends at their lane. I finished off the pizza, returned our dishes to the snack bar, and found a table at the end of the lane assigned to Dad's team where I could sit and watch.

It was great to see Dad relaxed and joking with the other guys. Dad worked so hard that I didn't get to see this side of him very often.

On my way back to the snack bar for another root beer I almost knocked a lady off her crutches. I was able to catch her arm to keep her from falling to the floor.

"I'm so sorry," I said.

She looked at me, stared actually, and smiled. "Can this be little Dué all grown up?"

Confused by another woman. Perhaps it is a virus. "I'm Dué Bonogura if that's who you mean."

She pointed to my chair. "Sit, please."

I watched her work the crutches around so she could take a seat next to me. She used one crutch like a hook to snag another chair and pull it over to serve as a foot rest for her cast.

"Hello, Dué, I am Laura." She extended her hand.

As we shook, she lowered her voice. "Other than your father, I like to think I was your mom's best friend."

The light went on in my brain. "Oh, Miss Laura, I remember now!"

She toyed with her hair. "I was a blonde when you knew me and that was years ago."

I thought all women wanted to be blonde—more confusion for me. "Well, I think your hair looks pretty. Cheryl has brown hair too."

She grinned at my expression. "And who might this Cheryl be? Someone your dad is dating?"

Clueless as I was and am, I did not realize that she was messing with me.

"She's a friend."

"Ummmm."

Was I going to spill my guts to this lady in a bowling alley? Well, maybe, but not right away.

Sensing my discomfort, she changed the focus of conversation to her own life. It didn't take long for her to hit the big topics. She had been living in Chicago attending law school at the time of Mom's accident. Until recently, she had worked as an assistant in the District Attorney's office.

"So, you're here for a visit."

"No, Dué, I'm home." Her smile brightened, took on life. "And what do you two handsome men do with yourselves?"

"Dad works. I mean he's there for whatever I need, but he works harder than any other dads I know." I pointed at the alley where his team was bowling. "This is the longest I've ever seen him relaxed."

Laura looked in that direction, nodded. "Even when we were kids, he was a serious guy." She tapped my shoulder with her fist. "People don't change very much, Dué. Look in the mirror. The man you see is pretty close to the man you'll be."

"That's depressing. You mean I am going to be this stupid for the rest of my life?"

A look of concern passed her face. "Don't say that. You seem bright and interesting. Are you having trouble in school?"

"No, school is doing great." I pointed at her. "You're the ones I'm stupid about."

For a moment her laughter drowned the sounds of the bowling. It was loud enough to catch Dad's attention. He turned, looked at us, and stared at Laura.

The expression on his face changed from curiosity to recognition to laughter. He did not jump over the back of the bowling lane, but his Brunswick was still in his hand when he reached our table.

"Laura?"

She opened her arms and Dad knelt to hug her.

Me? I was cool. I took the bowling ball out of his hand to keep him from breaking her back with it.

Both of them speaking at once, they launched an epic catch-up session. Unfortunately, it didn't last very long.

With a series of hoots, catcalls, and rude noises, Dad's teammates demanded he finish the game.

"Are you going to be here a while?" Dad asked.

Laura nodded.

"So we can talk after?"

"Sure, Pietro."

Dad turned toward the alley and got maybe three steps away before I busted him.

"Hey, Dad. You might want this." I held up the bowling ball I had taken from him.

His grin turned to a blush of embarrassment. It was hard to see on his dark Sicilian skin, but I knew it was there. Laura did, too.

When he finished the game, the three of us talked until the alley shut down for the night. Laura gave us a ride home. Dad invited her in for a beer, and they stayed in the kitchen talking for a long time. I remember hearing Dad laugh with her. That was an awesome sound.

Chapter 25

I picked up parts of the conversation because my bedroom was next to the kitchen. From what I heard, she had left New Orleans to attend law school in Chicago. I was probably five- or six-years-old then.

Around the time of Mom's accident Laura was in a program that allowed students who worked during the day to go to law school at night. She apologized to Dad for not dropping everything and coming back home to help him with Mom and me.

I think she cried a little about that because I remember hearing Dad's consoling tone of voice with her.

She finished law school and had to spend a few months studying for the Bar exam.

That sounded sort of dumb to me. She finished school, passed all the tests, and then had to take another exam?

Anyhow, she passed that and got a job as an assistant to the District Attorney. She got engaged to somebody up there, but when she got shot and they thought she might lose her foot, the guy left. Yeah, she got shot.

When she told the story to Dad, it sounded like something out of one of the "True Crime" magazines they have in the barbershop.

This all happened a few months earlier. Miss Laura was in the courtroom waiting her turn to present her case. She told Dad that even before the shooting she didn't think it was a great idea to have really bad criminals in the same room with people accused of minor crimes.

"Pietro, the man I was prosecuting was behind on his child support payments. The shooter was accused in a rape homicide. Oh, and he was nuts!"

"Laura, didn't they have him in handcuffs?" Dad asked.

"Sure they did, but, Pietro, have you ever seen the police on court house duty? These are the cops who can't or don't want to be on the street." She tried to suppress a giggle but was unsuccessful.

"The D.A. calls them the donut police. You know what I mean: overweight, out of shape, clocking time until their pensions start.

"There were two of them assigned to this perp. One turned to wave to a friend on the other side of the room. When he turned, his pistol was exposed and ready for the taking. I saw the whole thing happen.

"He shot the officer whose pistol he had taken, then the other one next to him. I suppose he was trying to create confusion so he could escape. He fired one shot in the direction of the judge and two other shots before the judge's bailiff shot him. The second shot was the one that got me."

I heard Dad express sympathy.

"I'm sure there was pain, but at that moment, all I knew was that I was on the floor and not sure why.

"The EMT's were terrific. I'd bet I was in the operating room within an hour of the shooting."

She went on to tell Dad how she wouldn't let them give her a general anesthetic right away because she was afraid they were going to amputate her foot. When they convinced her they would not do that without her consent, she let them operate.

"What's the prognosis on your foot?"

From her voice I could tell she was trying to sound upbeat. I would have been terrified. "Pietro, at least they aren't talking about having to amputate anymore."

Dad's voice sounded different, sort of hushed. "Thank God for that."

"Best case, I'll be able to walk without a cane or crutch. Worst case, I'll be on crutches or something like that forever." She paused. "But even in a best-case scenario, I'll never be able to fast dance again."

Dad blew me away with his answer—it was so un-dad. "As if you could before you got shot."

And then the two of them burst into laughter. I was confused, but I listened and learned.

From what I overheard, Laura went on a lot of dates with Mom and Dad. No, not like a double date. It was Mom, Dad, and Laura.

I found it hard to believe that she had trouble getting dates. Maybe she had not been very pretty as a teenager, but she was one awesome-looking lady.

When they went to dances, Dad would do all the slow dances with Mom and do the fast dances with Laura. Guess that was why Dad's joke cracked them up.

I heard Dad comment on the boyfriend who dumped her. "When we were kids, you were always so particular about the guys you dated. Heck, that's why so many of my dates with Chetta were with you, too."

"That was a bonus for you, Pietro. The two best-looking women on this side of town as your dates! But if I didn't think the guy would be as much fun as you two, I didn't want to waste my time."

"So how'd you end up with the loser in Chicago?"

"What makes you think he was a loser?"

"Because he walked out on you. Never mind that he walked out on you when you needed a friend. That just makes him a bigger loser. Laura, do you have any idea how lucky you were? Imagine if you had married him."

As I was slipping into sleep, I remembered something Dad had said at the bowling alley: he was not dating anyone and had no wish to do so.

There was a grin on my face as sleep hit. That may have been true before Laura arrived, but it didn't sound that way now. Go Dad!

Chapter 26

My paranoia woke me up around sunrise. Dad was sleeping. I left a note next to the coffee pot for him saying I had gone for a run.

My internal autopilot set a course for Cheryl's house. Maybe she'd see me jog past her window and wait on her porch for my return trip. No luck, but I thought I saw a couple of lights on. Someone was awake early on a Saturday morning, but the *Times-Picayune* remained on the front lawn. Odd.

I was home by seven-thirty to set the telephone vigil. If Dad noticed my anxiety, he didn't mention it. He drank a cup of coffee while he read the paper before leaving for his Saturday accounting job.

I reached for the phone to call her at nine, nine-fifteen, nine-thirty, and nine-forty-five. Each of those times, I was able to stop my hand from lifting the receiver. I made the call at ten. "Good morning, Mr. Wolf, it's Dué. Could I speak with Cheryl?"

I heard a female voice in the background. It sounded like Granny, but if it was, she was mighty upset.

"One second, please." I heard his hand cover the mouthpiece. After what seemed like the longest time, he spoke. "Dué, could you come over?"

"Is anything the matter?"

"Just come over."

There was something wrong! I could sense it from my conversation with Mr. Wolf, and I could feel it in my gut. The bike ride to her house was a blur. I didn't take the time to set my kickstand, but let the bike fall on her front lawn as I raced down the driveway to the back door. Cheryl's mom opened the screen door as I approached. Granny and Mr. Wolf were at the kitchen table. I was terrified. What was wrong?

"Sit down, Dué," Mr. Wolf said before I had a chance to speak. It was just as well. I was out of breath from the record-setting bike ride.

"Cheryl-Anne's date did not go very well," he said.

"That's a goddamn understatement," Granny said.

He admonished her with a look.

I was crazy with worry. "Is she hurt?"

"She's all right, but she is very upset."

Granny took control. "Son, be quiet." She turned toward me. "The brat she went out with was no gentleman. He tried to grope my baby, but she fought him."

I thought I was going to be sick. Granny read me. "No, Dué, it did not go any further than that, but like my son said, she is very upset."

I heard a sniffle from Cheryl's mom. "That is why we asked you to come over, Dué. She won't come out of her room and won't talk to any of us. We don't know what to do."

"Want to see if she'll talk to me?"

Her mom nodded. "Please."

On the way down the hall, the thought passed my mind that I might want to try some of Leo's training on Cheryl's date. I put that aside when I reached the door to her room.

I tapped on it. "Hey pal."

"Dué?"

"Yeah."

There was a space of perhaps an inch between the bottom of her door and the floor. I could hear footsteps as she walked across the room to the door. "Go home, Dué. I'll call you." I knew it was her, but the voice sounded different. Even though we were sort of alone, she wasn't using Anthony.

I sat on the floor next to the door and placed my fingers through the separation between the door and the floor. "Nope."

"Please, Dué. I don't want to talk to you."

"I know that, but I'm thinking that later on you might want me around. I'll wait."

I listened and heard her footsteps walk away, followed by the creak of her bed.

I had never been inside her room, but I had waited in the hall once while she picked up extra pencils for our homework. I remembered that her bed faced the door.

I wiggled my fingers. No response.

I wiggled them again and heard her move on the bed. I continued the wiggle.

"Dué!"

Even with the restricted movement, I had only an inch or so to work with. I made a waving motion with my finger-tips.

Her voice was calmer. "I appreciate what you're trying, but please go home."

"Can't do that."

"Why?"

"Cheryl, before she died, my mom taught me a lot. Ever since your folks—Granny, actually—gave me an idea of what happened, I've been thinking of something Mom said. She told Dad and me that the longer you wait to discuss a problem, the harder it gets to start. That's why I can't leave."

She didn't answer, but I heard a muffled sound. Perhaps she was crying into her pillow?

I continued. "It doesn't have to be with me. I could ask one of your folks or Granny."

For that suggestion, I got a definite "No."

But "no" was a word; we were talking.

"Could you come over to the door, please?" I asked.

"Why?"

"Because I'm selfish. It's tearing me up for you to be so sad and so far away."

"For heaven's sake, Dué, don't be so dramatic. I'm just on the other side of the room."

A whole sentence—I was making progress. And she moved. I heard the bed creak again followed by her footsteps. She sat on the floor next to the door. I felt her fingertips on mine. I enjoyed the moment in silence.

"Anthony," she whispered through the door. "I'm sorry."

Our fingertips remained in contact and she was using my name. This was good.

"Sorry for what?"

"That I'm being such a ninny."

"Hey," I said. "Nobody talks ugly about my girl. That includes you. How about you and I talk for a little while and then I'll leave?"

"Talk through the door?"

"Cheryl, talking through the door is too weird. It has to be in person."

"No!"

"Why not?"

I heard a sniffle. "Because I don't want you to see me."

"I can't think of any reason why I wouldn't want to see you."

"My eyes are all red and puffy."

I didn't reply.

"Anthony?"

I smiled. It was not a win yet, but we were talking. "Give me a second, I'm thinking."

The finger contact remained. "Thinking about what?"

"A way to solve this door thing." I paused. "Try this."

"What?"

"First of all, do you trust me to keep my word?"

She didn't hesitate. "Completely."

"What if I promised not to look at you? You could open the door and I could come in, sit on the floor and not look at you. I'd keep my eyes on the wall the whole time."

I could have been wrong, but I sensed a smile when she answered. "Anthony, that is a pretty dumb idea."

"As dumb as sitting on the floor on opposite sides of a door?"

She didn't answer, but her fingertips left mine and I heard movement on her side of the door. I stood.

The knob turned, the door opened.

True to my word, I edged into the room, careful not to look in her direction. I sat on the floor, yoga-style, faced the wall, and waited.

She was soft on her feet. I didn't know she was close until her hand touched my shoulder. "I don't know if I want to talk to your back."

"Ready for another brilliant idea?"

"How many do you have?"

There was definitely a smile in that sentence.

"Just one for now. Why don't you sit behind me, lean your back against mine? It would be like you were talking to yourself in the room, but you'd be able to feel me close to you."

"You are so silly." But she did as I suggested and sat behind me. When I felt her back lean against mine, I knew she was going to be fine.

"Could we start with me making a confession?" I asked.

"What do you mean?"

"Sometimes it's difficult to find the right place to open a story. My confession will help. You can start when the red Oldsmobile, Arkansas license 4826, parked in front of your house."

As quick as she was on the basketball court, I had never seen her move this fast. She leapt to her feet and slapped the back of my head. "You were spying on me? Out!" She opened the door with such force that it banged against the stop.

I shook my head. "Not until I tell you my story and you tell me yours."

"Your story?"

"Yep, so you can understand me and why I happened to be in the tree."

A long pause followed.

"You were in the tree across the street?"

"Come sit down like before. Please."

"No."

"Cheryl, this is embarrassing for me. Please." I can whine when required.

She sat behind me but left the bedroom door open.

"I know what we said about trust and all. And I do trust you. I trust you to keep the promise you made about telling me if you had a date and if you became interested in anyone. But, I have a huge imagination. I pictured your date as a good-looking rich athlete. I thought about him the whole day when you told me about the date, and the next day, too. Then I had a brilliant thought. If I could see him when he picked you up, maybe he'd be a real geek and

I wouldn't have to worry. So I ran over here, climbed the tree, and waited.

"When I saw him get out of the car and realized he was old enough to drive, I pretty much thought I was history. I climbed down from the tree and left."

I felt her relax against my back.

After a few minutes, she told me the story. I did not interrupt until the very end.

When Joel, that was his name, had come into the house, there had been a bit of a problem. Her parents had thought he was a year or two older, not four or five. Her parents had made Cheryl and Joel wait in the living room while they discussed the matter. Only because he would be driving directly to Mr. Wolf's friends' home did they allow her to go with him.

The grown-up party was in the front part of the large house. The kid party was in a room by their pool. Cheryl said it was called a gazebo.

She said she was uncomfortable as soon as they walked in the door. All of the boys and some of the girls were drinking beer. After the introductions they talked for a little while before he asked her to dance. At that point, to use her words, his hands "started to roam."

While not being specific about the target places for his hands, she said she was constantly pushing his hands away. He had told her to quit acting like a baby and had placed both of his hands on her bottom to pull her close. She had slapped him.

That is where I interrupted. "Good for you."

"No, Anthony. I was wearing a ring Granny had given me. When I slapped him, it cut his cheek. He yelled and pushed me. I tripped over a chair and fell down. I guess that scared me even more. I got up and ran to the main house. I was crying and asked the grown-ups to call my dad."

I could feel her back shake as she started to cry. I broke my promise about looking at the wall and turned to take her in my arms.

She did not object and buried her face in my chest. I petted her hair, told her how proud I was of her, and then I screwed up. I told her I loved her.

Those beautiful brown eyes, red-rimmed with tears, looked up at me. "Don't say that, Anthony."

"I can't apologize for saying something that's true."

"No, you're just making this harder."

As always, I was confused. "I don't understand. I thought I was helping."

Her head returned to its position close to my chest. "You're helping by being so sweet about what happened last night. But that just makes what I have to do that much harder."

I was back on that pogo stick bouncing around the minefield.

She pushed away from me, rubbed her eyes with her hands, and let out a deep breath. "I've been thinking about this all night and all morning. After last night, well, I've decided that I'm just too young to be dating."

Talk about a shot from out of nowhere!

I was completely, totally, one thousand percent not ready for that. I suppose I didn't handle it very well. "Does that mean no more you and me?"

She nodded, crying again. "I'm so sorry."

"Yeah, me too." I stood and left the room. I must have said something to her parents and Granny on the way out the door, but I have no idea what it was. To show how out of touch I was, I had walked to within a half block of my house before I realized I had ridden my bike to Cheryl's. I took some time to compose myself before making the return trip.

My bad luck held. Cheryl was sitting on the lawn by my bike. That shows how crappy life had become—thinking it was bad luck to see Cheryl.

"Dué, I'm sorry. I did it all wrong."

I picked up my bike, looked at her feet when I spoke. "Cheryl, I don't know much, but I don't think there's an easy way for you to tell me it's over."

"See, I told you I did it wrong. I didn't mean over like over forever. I meant that I need time. I need to grow up and learn how to handle dating things."

If it were not for the fact that I was crazy in love with her, I think I might have screamed at her. "Cheryl, since the day you asked me to your cousin's party and started all of this, I've been clueless. Nothing has changed—nothing except that I've never in my whole life felt better than when I'm with you.

"Ten minutes ago, you told me we were done. To me, that meant forever. Now you say, maybe not forever." I shook my head. "Call me when you decide what's next." I climbed on my bike.

"Wait, Dué."

"What?"

"I have a favor to ask."

Earlier, my answer would have been on the order of "whatever you need." Now I said, "What?"

"I really don't want anyone to know about what happened last night."

Shame on me. I said a cruel thing, but her words had hurt. "Cheryl, if you think you have to ask me to keep this quiet, it probably is a good idea for you to take a break from all of this."

Chapter 27

I have no memory of the ride home. I parked my bike in the shed, changed into a pair of shorts, and went for a run. I have no idea how far I ran—five or six miles, maybe more. I passed Grandma and Pappy's house on the way home and stopped in for a glass of water. I was so out of it that I didn't notice Laura's car in their driveway.

She waved when I walked into the kitchen. "Hi, Dué."

"Hi, Miss Laura."

"You seem surprised to see me here, Dué."

And then the most wonderful thing happened. Grandma smiled. She did not simply smile, she glowed as she placed her hand on Laura's. "Laura was like a second daughter to us, Dué. It's wonderful to have her back."

"Damn right," Pappy agreed.

I opened the refrigerator, poured a glass of cold water, and took a seat at the kitchen table across from Laura. As I did so, it hit me that this was the first time I had served myself anything at Grandma's. She and Pappy had waited on me like servants, and now Grandma was giving that attention to Laura. Was I spoiled? Of course. Was I jealous? Absolutely not. I hadn't seen a smile like that on her since, well, a very long time.

"Miss Laura, last night you said you had just gotten back to town."

"Correct, Dué, and good memory."

"Do you have a house here?"

"Not yet, Dué. I'm staying in a hotel while I look for a place to rent for a while."

Pappy stood. "I have two words. Both are 'No.'"

The three of us looked at him.

"The first 'no' is to the hotel. There's no way our favorite girl is going to stay in a hotel. There's a guest bedroom and bath in the back of this house. It's yours."

"But, Pappy," I interrupted, "maybe the hotel has a pool."

"You want to swim, boy? Wait a minute and I'll throw you in the lake."

Grandma and Laura laughed. I wasn't real sure he was kidding.

"Second 'no': you're not renting anyplace. The schoolteacher who rents the other side of this house is getting married. She's moving out next month. You stay with us until she leaves, and then you move in there."

Laura gave him a hard stare. It lasted until I heard him say a word I had never heard him say before. "Please?"

Laura smiled. "I might consider that, but I will pay rent."

"You work that out with my wife. Come on, Dué." He grabbed my arm and indicated I should follow him outside. As soon as we reached his shop, which had been the garage, he turned to me with the most fantastic smile. "Did you see your Grandma's face, boy?"

I nodded.

He looked up and spoke to God. "Sorry I was so mad at you. You took your time, but it looks like you finally came through. Thank you."

I was stunned. Pappy praying! Wow!

He spoke some more about how much a part of their lives Laura had been and how glad he was to see the spark she had put back in Grandma. I thought about telling him about the spark I had seen in Dad, but I decided to wait.

"Do you know about her operation?"

"I heard a few things while she and dad were talking. What do you think, Pappy? Is she going to be able to walk?"

"Probably. She won't know how well until they remove the cast, but she's hopeful. That's another reason for her to stay here. We can give her all the help she needs."

After a little while, Pappy and I returned to the kitchen. I said my goodbyes and continued my run home. During that run, I thought about the difference Miss Laura had made in Grandma, Pappy, and my Dad. She was one magical lady!

Dad was sitting in his chair on the porch when I returned. "Hope you didn't wear yourself out."

I shook my head. "Close. I wasn't paying attention and ended up at the lakefront."

He motioned with his index finger. "Have a seat."

I plopped down on the porch step. "I stopped for a glass of water with Grandma and Pappy. Guess who was there?"

He grinned. "It had to be Laura. She told me she was going to visit them first thing this morning. How were they?"

I laughed. "Grandma looked like she was at a birthday party and had just opened a big present."

"That's good, son. I had a feeling Laura would be a great thing for your grandparents."

"You should have seen Pappy! He told her she has to live in the apartment they have on the other side of their house. And get this, Dad—he prayed."

"What?"

"Yep. Remember when I told you about the night in the swamp when I heard him humming and realized it was a hymn?"

Dad nodded.

"Well, when he and I went to his workshop in the garage, he said a prayer of thanks for bringing Miss Laura to Grandma."

Dad laughed. "Just like Pappy, no mention of what her arrival did for him."

"I don't know, Dad. To me it looked like most of his happiness was seeing Grandma's reaction."

"The Irish have a saying, Dué. They say that when God gives you a huge hill to climb, He sometimes sends an angel to help you. Maybe Laura is that angel for them."

In an incredible burst of maturity, I did not tease Dad and ask him if maybe he liked the angel, too.

Dad changed the subject. "We received an important phone call while you were out."

I did the question thing with my shoulders and included the man with the no-clue-look I was perfecting

"Leo called. He wants you at City Park Stadium tomorrow at

eight sharp. There's what's called an 'open' track meet in the morning. Leo wants you to run in a couple of events."

"Did he say why?"

"He has a friend who happens to coach track at Jesuit High. Leo would like him to see you run.

"Jesuit! Dad, that's the rich kids' school. We can't afford that."

He shook his head. "Son, I appreciate your concern, but don't worry. Leo explained their scholarship program. The high schools are not allowed to give out athletic scholarships, but they can and do offer scholarships to academically qualified students who can't afford regular tuition."

"What's that mean, Dad? How does it work?"

"According to Leo, if someone has the grades to be accepted, the school has a limited number of scholarships. He is of the opinion that if the coach handles the application, there is good chance that you could get one of the scholarships."

"Wow!" Talk about dream time! Jesuit High was hands down the best education New Orleans had to offer. Doctors, lawyers, engineers, judges—whenever anybody important was in the paper, the article would mention that he was a Jesuit graduate.

Dad shook his head. "I always thought your talent at mathematics would be the door-opener for your life. Who would have thought it would be running?"

"I know I'm sort of fast, Dad, but I'll be surprised if I'm fast enough to impress a coach from Jesuit."

"Dué, Leo says it's more than just speed—he says you have a smooth gait. You give the impression that you could run forever."

It was my turn to laugh. "I thought the word 'gait' applied more to horses than people."

Dad winked. "Leo does live at the track. That place has its own language."

We celebrated by cooking chicken, sausage, and shrimp jambalaya. The whole Jesuit thing had me so excited that I had forgotten about Cheryl—that is, until I tried to sleep. While one part of my brain was in love, the other part missed the simplicity of my pre-Cheryl life.

Dad had said he'd wake me up in time to make it to the park, but it was Pappy who shook my shoulder and offered a cup of coffee. "Reveille, boy! Big things ahead for you!"

My great debut in the world of track and field hit a snag when we entered the stadium. I was wearing tennis shoes. All the other kids wore cleats. The official told me I could not participate.

Had it not been for the intervention of the Jesuit coach, I believe Pappy and Leo would have flipped a coin to see which one of them would have the privilege of kicking the official's butt.

Dad motioned for me to step aside with him and watch the discussions. The coach was super cool. He placed himself between Pappy, Leo, and the official and acted as a sort of mediator.

After everyone had his say, the coach closed the subject. "Let the kid run."

In order to demonstrate my stamina, Leo had entered me in two races that were about 30 minutes apart: the one-mile and the 5K, that's 3.1 miles.

I finished sixth out of the 20 who ran the mile. Since the other 19 kids in the race were high school freshman and sophomores, the coach was impressed. Leo pointed to his stopwatch and had a discussion with the coach about my time.

I finished third in the 5K. This time Leo and Pappy were looking at the stopwatch and jumping up and down like cheerleaders.

That night Dad told me what had them so excited: I had the same pace per mile in both events. "Leo says that's very important. There's a 12K next Saturday. He thinks you can nail down your spot at Jesuit if you do well in that race."

"Do I need cleats, Dad? I have some money saved."

He shook his head. "This is a road race. You run in the streets, no cleats. I want you to relax about the cleat thing. Pappy and I will make sure you have cleats for your next event at the track."

I looked at him.

"I wanted to buy them, but Pappy wants to feel a part of all this."

Chapter 28

A long time ago, a famous writer visited New Orleans. I think there is something about my city that draws writers and painters to us. Anyway, our cemeteries blew him away! He called them "cities of the dead." I think that is because most people get buried above the ground in little house-like things called mausoleums or tombs.

New Orleans people make a big deal of honoring the dead. Right before the first day of November, All Saints' Day, the cemeteries are busy places as family members clean and white-wash the tombs and gravesites.

When I was little, Aunt Rose, Aunt Na-ne, and I would get on the bus carrying all sorts of buckets, brushes, and other things to clean the family tomb for the holy day.

The cemetery where Mom was buried was about a 20-minute bike ride from our house. Dad and I visited on special days—her birthday, Christmas, like that. But now and again, a guy needed to talk to his mom.

Yeah, I know that God is everywhere, and if that's true, the saints are everywhere too. But there were times when I needed a stronger connection. What worked for me was to go to the tomb and place my hand on the letters of her name. When I sat like that, touching the name Conchetta, I felt like she could hear me.

I hadn't been to talk to her in a while, so I had a lot to say to bring her up to date.

I locked my bike to the fence and walked along the rows of tombs to Mom's. I stood in front of the granite and said a couple of prayers. The good part was next: I sat on the step and placed my hand on her name. The feel of the chiseled letters comforted me. I spoke to her.

There was so much to discuss: Father Pete, the creepy guy—I couldn't use the other name in front of Mom—Cheryl, Jesuit, my running, and Laura. It took a while to cover everything.

"Mom, you should have seen Grandma with Laura. Holy cow!

It wasn't like you were back. Nothing could be that great, but this was pretty good. Pappy even said a prayer of thanks. Can you imagine that?"

I was about to tell her how happy Dad seemed when I heard a sound. I turned and saw Laura coming down the path. I don't think she saw me because she moved with her head down, her eyes searching the ground before she moved her crutches across the uneven and sometimes broken pieces of sidewalk.

When I called her name, she was at first startled, but then she smiled. "Hello, Dué. Looks like we both wanted to talk to Chetta today."

"Hi, Miss Laura."

She sat next to me on the step in front of the tomb. "Do you come here very often?"

I shook my head. "Mostly the usual days, like her birthday and my birthday, but now and again, I make extra trips to visit."

"Does it help you to be here?"

I gave an embarrassed half-laugh. "It probably makes no sense, but when I talk to her while touching her name on the stone, well—"

She patted my hand. "Anything that gives you a close feeling to Chetta is a good thing."

I stood.

"Leaving?"

I nodded.

"Hopefully not on my account."

I shrugged. "Thought you would want to be alone with Mom."

Laura patted the step next to her. "No way, Dué. Sit with me. Your mother loved people around her, the more the better." She touched the name as I had, her fingers tracing the letters. "I'm rarely absolutely positive about anything, but I am a hundred percent sure that she is a happy spirit today as she sees her son and her best friend visiting this special place."

Laura took my hand and held it. "Do you talk to her or pray to her, Dué?"

"A little of both, I guess. Before you got here today, I was telling her about all the things that have gone on in my life these last few weeks."

She squeezed my hand. "You have been a busy young man."

I shook my head to disagree. "I haven't been busy on purpose. A lot has just happened around me."

"That's what makes great men and women, Dué. How well they react to life's situations." She patted Mom's name. "Chetta, this is nothing you don't know, but this young man has made you very proud."

She did a strange thing. She kissed her finger tips and transferred the kiss to the chiseled letters of Mom's name. "Chetta, if you have any pull up there, see if you can fix this foot so that I'm not a burden to anyone."

"I think Mom can handle that."

Laura laughed. "And what makes you so sure?"

It was my turn to touch her name. "She's in a favor-granting mood. She's getting me a shot at Jesuit. She sent you here to give Grandma and Pappy happiness."

"Anything else on your list?"

"Yes, Miss Laura, and it's a big favor. She needs to help me figure a way to keep Dad from working so hard."

"I don't mean to pry, Dué, but I have been thinking about that since you mentioned it at the bowling alley. I thought the police department paid well."

"I guess they do, but Dad said the medical bills were huge."

She seemed puzzled. "What medical bills? Has someone been sick?"

It was my turn to give her a look like she was maybe clueless. "Mom's bills."

"Chetta's bills?"

I nodded. "She was mostly in a coma from the time of the accident until she died."

"I knew that, but your dad shouldn't have to pay. The young man who hit her was drunk. He or his insurance should pay. Besides, if I remember correctly, he came from a wealthy family."

"Yeah, but he didn't have any insurance because he had been in trouble before. Dad said his family had done some lawyer thing where they were not responsible for him anymore."

"What! Did your dad talk to a lawyer?"

"Sure. But after he talked to him, Dad said he thought it would be easier to pay the bills than to maybe have to pay the bills and a lawyer."

She did a strange thing, given what we were talking about and all. She grinned. "Dué, I have no idea what the other lawyer said, but that is crazy. Besides, now your Dad has a lawyer who will work for hugs from his son." She placed her arm around my shoulders and gave me a squeeze. She released me and patted the tomb. "This, Chetta, is something I can fix. Let's go to work, Dué."

I helped her stand and we started to walk away. I had one of my brilliant thoughts and turned to face the tomb. "Hey, Mom, that sounds like a deal. You take care of Miss Laura's foot and she'll take care of Dad."

I looked at Miss Laura and saw a trace of color in her face, like a blush.

I realized she could have misunderstood what I said and clarified my statement. "I mean she'll take care of Dad's working so hard."

As we walked toward my bike and her car a small voice in the back of my brain told me my first statement may have been correct. I thought about it, nodded my head, and replied to the voice inside, "And that would not be a bad thing."

Chapter 29

Leo cut back on the defense training for the week so we could concentrate on running. His favorite exercise was to fill a knapsack with grain and oats from the horse feed sacks and have me run on the soft sod of the race track with the knapsack on my back, something he said he learned from the Marines.

While I had always been a guy who enjoyed sleep, and one who never had a problem falling into deep, restful sleep, that week found me hitting the pillow harder than ever before.

Leo had cancelled the after-school practice session Friday so I would be fresh for the big race on Saturday morning.

In addition to resting, an afternoon off would give me the chance to catch up on a reading assignment and book report I had been postponing.

I was curled up in bed reading a mystery when the phone rang.

"Bonogura residence, Dué speaking."

"Hello, Dué."

The voice needed no introduction. At that point in time, I had no idea what sultry meant, but she nailed it.

"Hi, Ashley."

"I'm flattered, Dué. You know my voice."

The proper response would have been "deaf people remember your voice," but I had better sense than to flirt with a flirt.

"What's up?" This was my first call from Ashley.

"Did you get the results of your social studies project back yet?"

"No. You?"

"Dué, I got an A plus. Mom was so excited she said I could have a party tonight. Would you like to come over?"

Going to a party at Ashley's would do nothing to help me get back into Cheryl's good graces. "Sorry, I can't make it."

"I think a favorite basketball player of ours is going to be disappointed."

I stalled for time, my brain moving faster than my feet on the track. "Cheryl's coming? That's nice."

"Has your answer changed?"

I laughed, working it out. Cheryl had not called to say we were back as boyfriend-girlfriend. I was thinking—never one of my strong points in this arena—no dancing with Cheryl, no hanging out with her, pretending we were just friends. This would not help me get any sleep before the big race. I thanked Ashley for asking, but said my answer was still "no thanks."

It wasn't the best plan. I wouldn't get to see her at the party. I would spend the night with visions of her dancing with my pals, now former pals, looking a lot cooler than they ever did in real life.

Miss Laura to the rescue! She called to ask Dad and me to join her at my grandparents' home for dinner. She was cooking a pizza recipe she had learned in Chicago. It was called "deep dish" pizza.

Chapter 30

The race was huge, like a Mardi Gras parade with runners, some in crazy costumes, and spectators scattered along the route. At the time I wasn't aware of it—probably a good thing for my nerves—but people travelled to New Orleans from all over to participate in the race that would one day become the French Quarter Classic.

The race also played a major part in setting the course of my life, but for me on that weekend, there were other important things.

The starting point was at the lakefront where Bayou St. John meets the levee. The finish line was at Jackson Square in the French Quarter. The course followed Bayou St. John to Orleans Avenue and through Mid-City and into the French Quarter. This was the longest distance I had run and I pushed myself really, really hard, sprinting wide open when we hit the Quarter and realized there was less than a mile to go. I was not sure how well I had done until I saw Pappy's face. He was yelling, crying, and hugging me all at the same time.

On the way home Pappy and I stopped at the K&B drug store, pulled Dad away from his weekend accounting job, and picked up Grandma and Miss Laura for a celebration lunch.

New Orleans is a terrific place to live for a bunch of reasons—not just Mardi Gras and food. Every neighborhood has its own awesome restaurants, but I guess those count as food. The place Pappy selected for lunch was not too far from the Track, the area he called his "stomping grounds."

Grandma was so happy talking to Laura that I don't think she noticed where we were. She didn't like anything about the racetrack.

Pappy knew the waiter. When asked the occasion, Pappy said, "Our boy finished thirty-fifth!"

"Is that something to brag about, Pappy?" I was not sure I understood.

"Boy, the ones who finished ahead of you were either professional runners or on college track teams. You beat every single high school kid in the city."

That was a bit of an exaggeration. Not every high school runner had entered the race, but it was still a big deal.

The menu was what I call "classic neighborhood Italian." To open we shared a huge "Wop Salad." That is like an antipasto salad with the salami and cheeses, but with added olive salad. The main course was spaghetti and meatballs. The meatballs had melted cheese centers. The sauce, which in New Orleans we call red gravy, was done Sicilian-style: rich, deep red, and sweet.

But here is what was incredible.

Grandma didn't drink and wasn't too happy with those who did. I know that it seems strange, given her feelings on that matter, that she married Pappy. I can't figure out my own generation—no point in trying to understand those who came before me.

Anyhow, this place is famous for having the coldest beer in the city. The beer is more than cold—it's just above freezing. The mugs are frozen, too. When the beer hits the mug, it sort of freezes to it and makes a coating of ice.

Laura turned to Grandma. "Watch this, Miss Chris."

Grandma's name was Christina, but Laura called her "Misschris," as if her name were two words in one. Laura used a spoon to scrape some of the frozen beer from the side of the mug and give it to Grandma to taste.

You should have seen look on Pappy's face when Grandma ordered a beer to share with Laura. They were like little kids with an ice cream sundae.

And Grandma was laughing and giggling like a schoolgirl.

Dad must have noticed the look of shock on my face. He called to me. "Dué." He winked and placed his finger to his lips.

At that moment, I believed in miracles.

We dropped Dad off at the drug store. As Pappy drove me home, he and I listened to the beautiful sound of Grandma and Laura laughing in the back seat of the car. Another strange thing happened. I looked over at Pappy and could have sworn I saw a tear roll down his cheek. He turned to me, winked, wiped his eye, and said, "Allergies."

I thought, "Baloney," but said nothing.

Aunt Rose greeted me at the front door with an envelope. "That pretty little girl who came to see you after the fight dropped this off for you."

I winced at the memory of the beating, thanked Aunt Rose, and carried the envelope to my room. I stared at it for a minute, not sure whether to treat it as a treasure or a bomb.

"Please call."

Still unsure of what it meant, I reached for the phone.

Granny answered.

"Hi," I said. "Is Cheryl home?"

Before Granny could respond, I heard a click as Cheryl picked up the phone in her room. Yeah, they had more than one phone in the house.

"I have it, Granny."

Not being sophisticated enough to wait for the click sound of Granny hanging up, I said, "Hi."

Silence for a couple of beats, and then Cheryl spoke, "Granny, I have it."

Click.

"Cheryl?"

"Yes, Dué. I was waiting for Granny to hang up the phone."

"Got your note."

"Thanks for calling. Your aunt said you were in a race this morning."

I nodded into the receiver. "Yes." I wasn't going to let myself get excited. She was using "Dué."

"It's past noon. Where'd you run from, Baton Rouge?"

My understanding of life was improving. That was her way of saying she had been waiting for my call.

"No, not from Baton Rouge, just a 12 kilometer run. I did okay and Pappy took Dad and me and Grandma and Laura out to eat to celebrate." If her brain had been on wheels, I swear I would have heard the screeching of brakes on her end of the line.

"Laura?"

"You don't know about Laura?"

Her "no" did not sound like things were too happy on her end of this conversation.

"Gosh, that shows it's been a while since we talked. She was a friend of my Mom's. She's a lawyer from Chicago, but she's moving back here."

I could be wrong, but I thought I heard some relief in her "Oh." She paused before getting to what I guessed was the purpose of the call. "I missed you at the party last night."

My first thought was to reply that I had missed her for the last several weeks, but I did not have that sort of courage. "I thought I should get to bed early to be rested for this race."

"Nice try, Dué, but you know I have an eleven o'clock curfew. You wouldn't have been out that late. What's your next excuse?"

"If you had asked me, I would have come, but I didn't know what to do. I thought maybe Ashley was messing with me."

"And?"

"I mean it's one thing seeing you at school, hello and all that. But to be at a party and not be able to ask you to dance and see you dancing with other guys, well, I didn't want to do that."

"And who said you couldn't ask me to dance?"

Sometimes I was on the pogo stick and didn't even know it. "Did I miss something? Didn't you say we weren't going to be boyfriend-girlfriend for a while?"

"That doesn't mean we can't dance together. It only means we wouldn't dance as close."

I couldn't think of anything to say. I said nothing but did think of banging my head against the wall to clear it.

"Dué, are you still on the line?"

"Yep, just had no idea what to say."

She chuckled. It was a good sound. "Now, there's a first for us, you with nothing to say. What are your plans for tomorrow?"

"I'm supposed to serve the 9:30 Mass. Nothing after that."

"We're going to 8:00 Mass. Why don't you come over to my house about 11:30? Maybe we could take a bike ride together."

I wondered if she could see my grin through the phone. "That would be great."

"Ask your dad if you can stay for a while, we have some things to discuss."

My grin went away, this was not good.

"And bring your appetite. I'll fix a snack for us."

My grin returned.

Chapter 31

At 11:30 the next morning, I set the kickstand on my bike in her driveway and knocked on the screen door.

Granny was in the kitchen. "Come in here, young man."

I walked across the linoleum floor to her chair. "Nice to see you, Granny."

"It's been a while. Have you grown?"

I laughed. "It's only been a couple of weeks."

"Three weeks, actually."

I turned to the sound of Cheryl's voice. You know what I was thinking—she was so pretty.

"Couple as in a figure of speech, meaning a few," I replied.

Cheryl crossed the room and walked toward me, very close, but we didn't touch. I could smell her, but maybe it was my imagination at work. "I'm so glad you came over."

"Thanks for the invite."

"If you two are going to be so formal, I'll leave." Granny stood from her chair and walked out of the room.

Cheryl was warm, friendly, and distant all at the same time. She acted excited as she told me what she had cooked for our snack— fried chicken and potato salad—but I felt like there was a shield around her. We kept our distance, even as we packed the picnic basket. She came close, but we never touched. It felt weird, but maybe I was imagining things. There's a big first.

Conversation flowed well as we pedaled toward Lake Pontchartrain. I asked her about basketball and her progress on the All-City Girls Team. For her part of the conversation, she seemed more interested in Leo's defense training than my running.

"I hope you realize you've changed," she said.

"What do you mean?"

"You're different."

"Dad said something along those lines. He and I talked about it."

"And?"

"Gee, Cheryl, this is embarrassing." I stopped my bike.

She pulled her bike next to mine, stopped, and did the look-through-her-eyelash thing. "And we're just starting."

I shrugged. "Maybe I should just go home."

She pedaled away and looked over her shoulder. "Be the biggest mistake of your life."

I said nothing until I caught up with her. "Biggest mistake of my life? You mean you packed some of Granny's rabbit stew in that basket?"

She leaned over and punched me on the arm, a hard punch, but delivered with a laugh.

"Now, continue. What did your dad think?"

"He said I was walking different. I thought it was from all the running, maybe my leg muscles were hurting or getting stronger, something like that. Dad said it wasn't just the way I moved. He thought it was an attitude thing."

Cheryl nodded.

"After the beating I took from Joey, I was pretty timid and scared. Dad said that's changed since my training with Leo."

"That's it, Anthony. It's not a swagger or anything like that, but you have this air of confidence about you."

I was embarrassed and used my usual defense tactic, a joke. "Hey, you really liked me when I was a wimpy math geek. Maybe I should go back to that?"

She let that comment slide and returned to questions about Leo and the defense training. We talked about a lot, but Jesuit High and my running were left out of the conversation.

We reached the levee, a mini-hill of grass-covered earth whose job was to protect us from any hurricane-driven tidal surge from Lake Pontchartrain. Rising to 16 feet above the rest of the land, it was a great place to hang out. In good weather there would be little kids sliding down the "hill" on pieces of cardboard, families using the constant breezes caused by the meeting of land and water to fly kites, and people on picnics like Cheryl and me.

We found a clear spot, spread the tablecloth, and arranged our meal. We worked together, but other than her earlier punch, there was no direct physical contact. I watched her arrange our dishes and thought of what Dad had said to prepare me.

"Son, if a woman decides to love you, you have to really screw up to lose her. Conversely, if she decides to dump you, no amount of pleading will help." He had paused and laughed. "Having said all of that, I'd like to quote Pappy. 'If you meet a man who claims to know anything about women, call him a liar and then write down everything he says.'"

"Why write it down if you think he's wrong?" I'd asked.

"Because, once again stealing words from Pappy, 'Somebody's got to understand them.'" He had closed with this last bit of wisdom. "If she starts to talk about just being friends, be a man, take it on the chin. It's over."

I enjoyed the meal, inhaled the pleasure of her company and waited for the jury's verdict.

She interrupted my praise for the food. "Watching you eat is all the compliment I need."

"How about I tell you how much I appreciate the effort?"

"That's allowed. It was my pleasure. Now, let's talk." She faced me, sat yoga-fashion on the other side of the tablecloth.

I had stretched out, turned to face her, and propped by head on my arm. "Guess you go first."

"While I was at the party, which you missed—but I believe we've been over that—Mick and Jimmy mentioned the running thing and the Jesuit coach."

Before I could reply, she said, "Not one of your friends asked me to dance."

"That's not what I was going to ask. I wanted to know what Tony had to say about it."

"He had nothing to say because he was never more than a foot away from Ashley."

In a life-saving moment, I did not ask if anyone could blame him for that.

She continued. "Jesuit has a program that starts in eighth grade?"

I nodded.

"So if they accept you, this is it. You'll be gone." She turned away from me. "That makes this conversation pointless."

"Cheryl, there are lots of times when I'm slow to follow our conversations, but this may be a winner. I am not moving, just going to a different school."

Her head remained turned. "But you'll meet someone else."

I slapped my head in exasperation. "Cheryl, Jesuit is an all-boy school."

She faced me but kept her eyes low. "I know that. But those boys will have sisters. Their sisters will have friends."

"Cheryl, until three weeks ago, you were the only girl I ever cared for."

"And now?"

"That's why we're here—to see what you want to do."

"The last time we talked you said you loved me. Do you still feel the same?"

"I've thought about that a lot these last few weeks, especially when I'm on the track or in a race. Running lets you clear your mind and concentrate on one thing. I have no idea what love means, but I know that I'm happy with you and miserable without you. Whatever that is, it's what I feel for you and it hasn't changed over these last three weeks."

I rolled over on my back, watched the low, puffy, cumulus clouds race across the sky.

"Anthony, a week after that thing, I had a talk with Granny. She asked me if I trusted you. I told her I did. Then she asked me why I had sent a boy I trusted away because a jerk I did not know had behaved badly."

I nodded, still watching the sky. "I always liked Granny."

"See, that's the thing. I didn't handle that situation very well."

I interrupted her. "Bull. You got him to stop whatever he was trying and you let everyone know he was an idiot."

"I think I could have done it differently, but that's where you come in. How would I act if you tried something like that?"

I rolled to my side to look at her. "That will never happen."

She gave a bitter half-laugh. "Sure."

"Listen to me. I said *never!*"

In the same tone, she said, "And you never think of things like that?"

I gave her my best smile. "Cheryl, if you had any idea of how often I think of you, all of you, you would be on your bike pedaling home."

Her blush was beautiful, redder than the pimientos in the potato salad.

"Before you run away, hear me out. The reason that would never happen is that I couldn't stand the thought of having done something that would make you stop seeing me."

"So if we got back together we'd stay just like we were?"

I reached for my tea and took a sip. "This may be the longest serious conversation of my life."

She was silent.

"My life was all about fishing and hanging out with the guys until you opened a new door. You asked me to the party, taught me to dance, and a kiss happened. No idea whose idea it was, but it seemed to be what you and I wanted to do.

"It would be cool to go along like that, only taking steps when we were both ready. But I promise you this, and do so with all my heart. If I ever misread you and take a bad step, the word 'no' will stop it."

I turned in her direction. Strange, she had moved closer, but I hadn't sensed it—too busy talking, I guessed.

Her voice was soft. "So if I hear what you're saying, the best way for me to be safe is to date you and only you."

"I like that plan," I said, wisely resisting the impulse to stand up and cheer.

She was quiet as was I.

The gulls were fighting over a piece of food they had discovered at a nearby picnic site. A sailboat with sails as white as the clouds cruised near the seawall.

"Anthony." Her voice was a whisper.

I turned. She was looking at me through her lashes and using

"Anthony." This was always a good thing. "Is there something you'd like to do?"

I nodded, made my hand into a fist and reached for hers.

She brushed it aside, leaned over and placed her lips on mine.

I don't know the physics of the moves, but somehow she moved from a seated cross-legged yoga position to being nose to nose and toes to toes next to me. Our arms wrapped around each other. And as the kiss continued, her lips parted ever so slightly. I felt the tip of her tongue brush my lips. Nothing in life would ever match that thrill.

Some time passed before we broke the kiss. When we did pull apart, both of us were flushed and breathing hard. She placed her face on my shoulder. "Anthony, I think we have to be very careful with that."

I nodded. "Me too. That is something we probably shouldn't try again for, oh heck, at least three or four minutes."

She punched me in the stomach. We laughed, giggled, tickled, hugged, and watched the boat sail on our lake.

Life was spectacular!

Chapter 32

And as great as life was at the Lake with Cheryl, it got even better. Instead of dinner being Dad and me, which was cool don't get me wrong, meals were now a family thing. Some afternoons, Laura would come to the house and she would join Aunt Rose and Aunt Na-ne in the cooking. Other nights, we would end up having dinner with Grandma and Pappy. And, of course, Laura would be there, too.

On this particular night, Dad was going to run a little late at work, and Laura had asked Cheryl's parents if she could join us for dinner with Grandma and Pappy. The dish was "Sticky Chicken," a sort of stewed chicken in rich brown gravy with onions and potatoes. Grandma's gravies were beyond description. I had a thought! If I could get Grandma to teach Cheryl's Granny how to make that gravy for her rabbit, or have her teach Grandma how to cook the rabbit in Grandma's gravy, it would be the most awesome meal ever.

After dinner, Pappy had asked Laura how Dad's case was coming along.

"Things are very interesting, Pappy." Yep, that what's she called him—everybody did, even Grandma. "Under normal circumstances in Louisiana, you have one year to file a lawsuit. But that does not apply when fraud is involved, as is the case here. The first lawyer Pietro talked to was wrong. The driver was living at home at the time of the accident. His parents had removed him from their insurance because of his earlier drunk driving accidents. They should not have allowed him to drive."

"Does he still live it home?" I asked.

She nodded. "That is interesting, Dué. It seems that the young man was mugged a year or so after the accident. He was pushed down a flight of stairs and is partially paralyzed. He spent a couple of years in a private hospital, but he is at home now. His parents added a room to the rear of their home where he and his caretaker live."

When Laura said that, I looked at Pappy.

His face was blank, and he lowered his eyes to stare at a place on the floor.

I watched him and wondered. A question formed which I could never ask.

Laura missed or ignored Pappy's reaction. "The fact is that regardless of whatever the first lawyer said, his parents supported him before, during, and after the accident. They are liable. Anything they claimed to have filed was no more than a sham, and therein lies the fraud. I have a second meeting with their attorney next week."

That was a new word for me. "What's a sham?"

Pappy spoke before Laura. "You can work on my grandson's vocabulary later. How'd the first meeting go?"

"To help give you a feel for the situation, you have to understand the wealth and social standing of this family. In the first meeting, I explained to their attorney that I would feel very confident bringing the case to a jury. A case where the actions of a teenage driver, driving under the influence as documented in the police reports, caused the death of a young mother. The driver had no insurance because of previous problems with alcohol, which had increased the premiums beyond which his parents were willing to pay. He was, however, driving one of his parents' cars. The widower not only has the task of raising his son as a single parent, but he has to work extra jobs to pay off his deceased wife's medical bills."

"Oh," and she smiled a very vicious smile. I never thought a smile could be vicious, but this one was. It must be something they learn in law school.

"This wealthy family has never offered a dime to help. The opposing counsel started to fold before I had a chance to mention how much the papers would enjoy seeing a past king of Mardi Gras accused of such actions."

"So you think Pietro will catch a break on this?"

Laura's smile was softer for this answer. "Nothing is sure until it is done, but I am absolutely certain all the bills will be covered. That means what he has paid and what is still owed. The only question is how much they are going to offer over and above that. Keep in mind there is only one section of the *Picayune* where these people want to be seen, the Society pages."

I raised my hand to speak.

Grandma asked me to wait. She had a question. She pointed at Cheryl's foot. "When did you get that cast? It looks new. What does that mean?"

Before she could answer, Dad tapped on the screen door and opened it. "Hey, I sure hope somebody saved some of that chicken for me?"

Laura looked at him and this was a beautiful smile. "Now, Pietro?"

With a grin, which threatened to split his cheeks, Dad said, "Go for it."

Laura stood, rested the cane she had been using aside, and walked to the stove to fix a plate for Dad.

Tears streamed down Grandma's face, Pappy stood and cheered. Cheryl and I applauded like we were at a school play.

After Laura placed the plate in front of Dad, she explained that she had graduated to a walking cast, which meant her prognosis was great. "Pietro and I wanted to surprise you."

While she was speaking, Cheryl pinched me. I looked at her with my usual question mark expression. She mouthed, "Watch Laura's hand."

I shifted my gaze to Laura and Dad. He was eating and while she spoke to Grandma and Pappy about her physical therapy, her hand remained on his shoulder.

I wasn't surprised. Laura was at the house a lot and their "talks" had moved from the kitchen, which was located next to my room, to the front room. And, those talks were pretty quiet.

"A sham?" I asked, trying to get back to my earlier question.

Laura looked at me. "You have been very patient Dué. Let's see if I can give you an example." She paused as if in thought. "Suppose a girl was a brilliant student."

I interrupted. "I know one like that."

Cheryl grinned.

And just suppose this brilliant young lady was interested in a young man who did very well in Spanish class. If she were to pretend to need help in Spanish in order to spend time with the young man that would be a sham. Understand?"

I looked at Cheryl who was blushing really, really red. I turned to face Laura. "I guess so, but I'm not sure. We don't take Spanish until high school."

Laura howled, Cheryl groaned and dropped her head to the table.

Dad's laughter rocked the room. "That's my boy!"

I stood, pointed at them and yelled, "Gotcha!"

The End

I hope you have enjoyed your time with Dué and his family. I have written another story, which is scheduled to be available as an eBook. You just might find it interesting.

Meet John Dees, a former naval aviator, veteran of the Iraq war, a man on a mission. A promise made to the memory of a friend brings him to the small Louisiana town of St. Francisville. The pledge was a simple one. He would care for the fallen comrad's family—a widow and a five-year-old girl. Watch how the child, Gabrielle, changes John's mission from caretaker to a quest for a princess, not just any princess, but a Fairy Princess.

The Pilot and the Fairy Princess
Chapter 1

The one-legged man pedaled his bicycle along a winding, tree-shaded lane on a mission to make amends—to fulfill the pledge he had made to "Duke."

His mouth formed a crooked grin. "Here I am, Duke." He spoke to the memory of his friend, the other pilot who had flown in the combat formation with him—the man whose death he knew he had caused in the lead-filled skies over Iraq. "Gonna give it my best shot."

He had arrived in Saint Francisville, Louisiana, the previous month and had used the time to locate a small apartment and explore the neighborhood. He had tried to find a way to introduce himself to Duke's widow. It had to be perfect.

"Hi Louise. I'm Toad, Duke's wingman. I'm the guy who knocked your husband out of the sky." He smiled. It was not a pretty smile. "Nope, that wasn't going to cut it."

He had planned to apply for a job at St. Mary's, the only Catholic school in town. He knew Duke's daughter would start kindergarten in the fall. Duke's strong religious convictions made it the obvious choice. With a voice full of cynicism, he had said to the walls of his room, "You are one awesome detective."

He had hoped to meet and befriend Louise in the capacity of teacher, coach, or school janitor, anything available at St. Mary's. In the small-town atmosphere of St. Francisville, a job at the school could place him within her circle of acquaintances. He would be in a position to know if Louise or her daughter were in need of any sort of assistance.

That was the pledge he had made during his parachute ride into the arms of Saddam's followers. "Can't bring you back, Duke, but if I get out of this, I'll make sure your wife and baby girl want for nothing."

The ad he saw in the local weekly paper had been a good sign. "Handyman needed for summer work." He had recognized the phone number from his notes, had dialed it and had spoken with Louise to arrange an appointment. He was pleased with his story. "Just moved into the area, hope for a teaching job when school starts, sure could use some summer work."

The branches of the live oaks formed a canopy over the road. He followed the directions she had provided and saw the white mailbox marker. Louise had described it as her driveway, but to a city-bred man, it was more of a street. Twenty-five yards down the drive, he pedaled into a clearing and saw the home—a white Victorian surrounded by deep porches which he had learned were called galleries in this part of Louisiana. He studied the home for a few minutes before he continued on to the house.

He stopped the bike, dismounted with a great deal of caution and set the kickstand. It would not do for him to fall on his face at the first meeting. He and his prosthesis were making progress in developing a relationship, but it was a slow process.

Louise and Gabrielle were seated on a swing in the center of a spacious porch. He removed his cane from the handlebar, offered a smile and moved toward the steps. "Had to be steps," he thought.

He negotiated that barrier successfully. "Good morning. Thank you for seeing me."

He could tell that Louise was making an effort not to look at the cane. It was what everyone did.

"Nice of you to come out—I'm Louise. This is my daughter Gabrielle." She extended her hand.

The introduction was the first test. Navy pilots' call-signs become their names. She should know her husband's wingman as "Toad." If John Dees struck a memory chord, there could be a problem.

"John Dees," he said taking her hand.

Before Louise could respond, Gabrielle broke into the conversation with the directness of a five-year-old. "Why do you walk with a stick?

"Cause half my leg is in an incinerator somewhere," did not make it beyond subconscious thought. "I hurt my leg and the stick keeps me from falling," he said with a wink.

Louise mouthed, "Sorry."

He shook his head. "Not a problem."

"How did you hurt your leg?" Gabrielle was not going to let it go.

Louise attempted to say something, but John was quicker. "I fell down and it broke."

She made a hurt face. "Oh. I'm so sorry. Will it get better?"

He repeated what the physical therapist had said to him about the prosthesis. He omitted the perky smile, which had accompanied the prognosis. "It will be better than new one day."

For the moment, Gabrielle was out of questions. She glanced at her mother for approval and switched from child to Southern hostess. "May I offer you some iced tea?"

He smiled and said that would be fine.

"Can I get it Momma?"

Louise nodded. "Yes you may. Careful, use two hands."

Gabrielle disappeared behind the screen door. Louise offered John a seat on the wicker rocking chair across from the swing. He accepted. "You have a beautiful home. When I first saw it, I thought I had fallen back in time, like back to the Civil War."

Her reply was a smile followed by a silence, which could have been but was not uncomfortable. After a few moments, she sighed. "There is so much to do here."

He nodded.

"I don't mean to be rude, but…"

He held up his hand. "You're not being rude. You want to know if I can do the job." He looked at the screen to make sure the little girl was out of earshot. He tapped the prosthesis with his cane. "I'm a vet, left part of the leg in the desert. I can pretty much do what a whole man can, just takes me a little longer."

Gabrielle returned to the porch with a full glass of iced tea and a smile of pride. "I remembered the napkin, Momma."

He accepted the glass, thanked Gabrielle, sipped the tea and smiled. "Can't get this anyplace but in the South—sweet tea."

"I get the mint from a garden Momma and I made," Gabrielle said. "Would you like to see it?"

He raised his eyebrows in question.

Louise offered a tired smile and nodded. "She sort of takes charge. Her father was like that."

"I know," came to John's lips. He swallowed the words, stood, and followed Gabrielle to her garden.

She pointed at the mint. "Momma says I have to cut it back."

Using the cane for balance, he crouched down and examined the plant. He pinched a leaf and smiled at the clean aroma.

Gabrielle was a storehouse of information about the grounds, house, and "barn thing" in the back. "All of this was my Granny's," she said.

"And now it belongs to you?" John smiled the question.

"Nope. It's all Momma's," she answered as her mini-tour concluded at the front of the house.

"Gabrielle, would you go inside and draw a pretty picture for Mr. John," Louise said.

Gabrielle offered a wise nod. "Means grown-up talk."

He laughed. "You are a trip, young lady."

She paused at the door. "What's a trip?"

"A most pleasant experience," John said.

Gabrielle followed the instructions and walked inside. John turned to face Louise. He looked into her eyes and saw sadness in the brown depths. "Don't know how the interview is going with

151

you, but I think the Boss likes me."

He remembered her beauty from the photograph Duke had kept on his desk, but he read fatigue and loneliness in the face before him. She said nothing and John felt she was searching for a pleasant way to say, "No thanks." That would not do.

"Might I make you an offer?" John asked.

She nodded. "Sure."

"How about you give me a trial period—a test? I'll spend the day working on the grass. End of the day, you feel I'm not the man for the job, I'll leave and you get the grass cut for free."

The same sad smile he had seen earlier crossed her lips. "You really want this job." It was both a question and a statement.

He stood. "Where's the lawn mower?"

She acquiesced. "In the barn, but it has not run in a long time."

He offered a wink. "I do mechanical."